FROM THE
NANCY DREW FILES

THE CASE: Nancy investigates the kidnapping of pitcher Sean Reeves's five-year-old daughter.

CONTACT: The Falcons' catcher, Luke Darlington, urges Nancy to take the lead on the investigation team.

SUSPECTS: Stormy Tarver—The owner of the rival Rangers, she's determined to win the championship at any cost.

Bert and Stella Zabowski—Sean's in-laws may be willing to go outside the law in order to gain custody of their grandchild.

Rebecca Carter—Caitlin's baby-sitter is desperate for money, and Sean's multi-million-dollar contract makes him a perfect target.

COMPLICATIONS: Absolute confidentiality is crucial to Nancy's case. But if reporter Brenda Carlton gets wind of the kidnapping story, the secret could end up on the front page of her newspaper.

Books in The Nancy Drew Files® Series

Available from ARCHWAY Paperbacks

Case 97

Squeeze Play

Carolyn Keene

AN ARCHWAY PAPERBACK
Published by POCKET BOOKS
New York   London   Toronto   Sydney   Tokyo   Singapore

This book is a work of fiction. Names, characters, places and
incidents are products of the author's imagination or are used
fictitiously. Any resemblance to actual events or locales or persons,
living or dead, is entirely coincidental.

AN ARCHWAY PAPERBACK *Original*

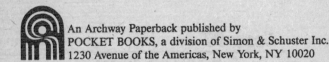

An Archway Paperback published by
POCKET BOOKS, a division of Simon & Schuster Inc.
1230 Avenue of the Americas, New York, NY 10020

Copyright © 1994 by Simon & Schuster Inc.
Produced by Mega-Books of New York, Inc.

ISBN: 0-671-79489-2

First Archway Paperback printing July 1994

10 9 8 7 6 5 4 3 2 1

NANCY DREW, AN ARCHWAY PAPERBACK and colophon
are registered trademarks of Simon & Schuster Inc.

THE NANCY DREW FILES is a trademark
of Simon & Schuster Inc.

Cover art by Cliff Miller

Printed in the U.S.A.

IL 6+

Squeeze Play

Chapter

One

ISN'T IT EXCITING, Nancy!" Bess Marvin practically sang the words, her long blond hair streaming back in the breeze. Even though it was a hot late-summer afternoon, the girls had turned the air conditioning off so the ride wouldn't feel claustrophobic. They were on their way to a baseball game a few miles away. "Three hours from now we'll be eating pizza with the next great catcher of the major leagues."

From the driver's seat of her blue Mustang, Nancy Drew grinned but kept her eyes on the road. "Luke Darlington has a way to go before he makes it into the Baseball Hall of Fame," Nancy said. "I bet he's still the same redheaded, freckle-faced kid we knew in school."

"He is, and he isn't," Bess's cousin, George Fayne, said from the backseat. "His freckles are still there, and his hair's still red, but he's different somehow."

Nancy caught a glimpse of George's face in the rearview mirror. Her dark eyes were focused someplace in the distance. Tall and athletic, she was much less flirtatious than Bess, which was why Nancy always paid close attention when George showed interest in a guy.

Luke Darlington had graduated from River Heights High two years before Nancy, George, and Bess. He had been playing baseball in the minor leagues since then and had been traded to River Heights's AAA team just a month earlier. Nancy and George had been in Japan at the time, solving a mystery. When they'd arrived home, they'd been delighted to learn that Luke was now playing with the River Heights Falcons.

"Tell me again about running into him and getting the tickets," Bess begged, throwing one arm over the back of her seat as she spoke to George. "Were there any other players with him? Like Sean Reeves? He is so awesome! I'd die to meet him."

Nancy was surprised that Bess even knew the name of the famous relief pitcher Sean Reeves. But then, she remembered, Bess had started working at the concession stand at the Falcons' stadium the night before. Obviously Bess would have picked up the name of one of the best-looking players in baseball.

"As I already told you, I ran into Luke at the

mall," George replied. "We talked for a while about his moving back here. He said he could get tickets for us—and, no, Sean Reeves wasn't with him."

"I hope Reeves plays today," Nancy said, brushing back her shoulder-length, reddish blonde hair. "He's supposed to have the best knuckleball in baseball."

"And the best relief record in the majors," Bess said, showing off her new knowledge.

A relief pitcher had the job of finishing a ball game when the starting pitcher tired or began pitching badly.

"Do you think it's true Sean was dropped down to the minors so the Falcons could win the AAA championship?" Bess asked over her shoulder.

"I don't really think so," George said. "The last two games he pitched in the majors were really bad. I think they sent him down for a tune-up. The owners probably hope to get him playing better before the major league playoffs this fall."

"Well, he was in tune last night," Bess said with a smile. Bess had told Nancy and George how Sean had come into the game in the seventh inning the night before. His pitching had helped the Falcons come from behind to beat the Mill City Rangers in the first game of their five-game series that would decide the league championship.

"Watch out for that—" George's words were drowned out by the sound of squealing tires as a concrete-mixing truck skidded into the intersection just ahead of them.

Nancy had already spotted the truck and swerved quickly to the right to avoid a collision, then eased the wheel back to the left to avoid skidding.

"Where did that guy get his license?" Bess said, shaking her head.

When Nancy arrived at the stadium, which was known as "the Roost," the lot was still mostly empty. She found a spot close to the entrance.

Next to her, Bess was nervously checking her watch. "I've got five minutes to get there," she said, adjusting the clasp that held her ponytail. "I'm supposed to be at the concession stand at one-fifteen sharp." Bess jumped out of the car and led her more athletic friends to the entrance. Though Bess was on the verge of being late, Nancy and George were early for the two o'clock game.

Bess showed her employee's pass as Nancy and George presented tickets stamped complimentary.

"Friends of a player?" the ticket taker asked.

"Yes, Luke Darlington," George said, her dark eyes sparkling.

"Oh, one of the new guys," the man replied, handing back their ticket stubs.

Within minutes the girls had reached the concession stand Bess was to work. It was tucked under the seats on the visiting team's side of the field. Nancy and George stayed long enough to buy the first hot dogs off the grill and to compliment Bess on her blue Falcon shirt and green apron. Then they agreed to meet by the Falcons' locker room after the game.

Nancy and George headed down the wide concrete passageway lined with concession stands. When they came to a stand that sold Ranger and Falcon souvenirs, Nancy stopped. "I'll have a Falcon button," she told the clerk. "One with the feathers." She handed the girl two dollars and took a pin with a picture of the Falcons' comical mascot on the front and a half circle of fluffy blue feathers around the top edge.

"A program and a button for me, too," George said, taking out her wallet. "It's the least I can do to show Luke I'm a fan."

"Tell me the truth about you and Luke," Nancy said, watching George's dark eyes.

"Now, Nancy"—George shook her finger playfully—"don't start questioning me like one of your suspects." George had helped Nancy solve many mysteries and knew better than to let herself be grilled by the ace teen detective.

"But you *are* a suspect," Nancy said, trying to sound mysterious. "You show all the signs of being interested in a certain Falcon catcher."

"We're just friends," George said, moving up

the ramp that led outside to the seats. "There we are," she said, pointing.

"Wow, he must really like you," Nancy said. "These are in the front row!"

George was smiling as the girls sat down.

Nancy wished that her boyfriend, Ned Nickerson, was with them. He had been gone for three weeks, working as a volunteer at a youth basketball camp sponsored by his college athletics department. Nancy missed him, but considering how often he had to be understanding of her work, she knew she had to be understanding of his.

On the field the Falcons and Rangers were warming up, and Nancy used her binoculars to focus on Luke Darlington's face. He was number 12 on the Falcon team.

"There's Reeves," George said, pointing to the Falcons' pitcher. "He *is* handsome."

"And a millionaire, from what I hear," Nancy added. "His last contract with the Captains, his major league team, was for $2.2 million for two years."

"I can understand the Rangers' owner being mad when the Captains moved a major league player down to their top farm team just in time for the championships. Even playing badly, he could be a real threat in the minor leagues," George said.

"Are an AAA team, a farm team, and a minor league team all the same?" Nancy asked.

"Pretty much," George answered. "Triple A ball is the best, and every major league is affiliated with a Triple A team. Most major league players spend some time on a farm team before moving up. Also, guys are sent back down to the minors when they're in slumps to work out their problems."

Nancy watched as the teams cleared the field for the start of the game. Unlike their opponents, the Falcons had never won a league championship, and no one expected them to beat the Rangers—until Sean had arrived.

"The Falcons'll be heroes in River Heights if they win the championship," Nancy said. As she spoke, the Falcon players were introduced one at a time, and the River Heights side of the stadium erupted in cheers.

"I know you're right," George said, surveying the crowd. "And Stormy Tarver would be green with envy."

George pointed toward a box across the stadium. Stormy Tarver, the Rangers' owner, was arriving just in time for the national anthem. Her short bleached-blond hair and large-boned frame made her easy to spot. Nancy saw her stop on the walkway beside her box, holding a cushion and thermos. She stood at attention until the anthem was over. Then Stormy tossed her things over the railing into the reserved box and turned to lead the Ranger fans in a cheer.

"She's really something," Nancy said, adjusting the focus on her binoculars. "Once in Mill City she went out on the field to argue with an umpire."

"Nobody likes to win as much as Stormy," George commented. "I wonder why she was late. She usually arrives half an hour before the game starts to fire up the fans."

"Maybe she was checking out the city's water mains," Nancy said, her blue eyes sparkling.

George laughed. The day before the championship was to start, a water main had broken and flooded the Rangers' stadium in Mill City, turning the infield into a muddy mess. The story had been reported complete with pictures of Stormy in big rubber boots wading through several inches of water where home plate was supposed to be.

"She didn't look very happy in the paper," Nancy said, still watching Stormy across the stadium.

"No, but the water break was good luck for us," George said. "She had to agree to play all five games of the series here in River Heights. Her field won't be ready to use for weeks."

The first five innings of the game turned out to be a slug fest, with the Falcons and Rangers each scoring four runs apiece.

The Falcons' starting pitcher was Rod Sanders, a long-time River Heights favorite.

"I think Sanders needs a rest," George said as a Ranger batter connected with one of Sanders's pitches to score another run.

Nancy sighed as the runner crossed home plate. "That puts the Rangers up one. If the Falcons are going to win this series, they're going to have to do better than this."

As Nancy spoke, a low chant started in the Falcons' front section and got louder as it spread back. Soon the stadium resounded with cries of "Bring on the Show! Bring on the Show!" and the sound of stomping feet.

Nancy and George looked at each other. It was hard not to get caught up in the cheer, but Nancy felt bad for the pitcher who was struggling on the mound.

"Rod used to be the most popular pitcher in River Heights," George said. "Now everybody wants Showboat Sean Reeves."

The fans got their wish in the seventh inning, when Showboat Sean strode out to the pitcher's mound.

"He saved the game yesterday," Nancy said. "Maybe he can do it again."

Sean held the Rangers scoreless in the seventh inning, and the Falcons made two more runs to go ahead 6–5. Victory fever swept through the crowd.

"Showboat! Showboat!" The calls rose joyously from the Falcon stands as the tall, handsome Sean Reeves jogged toward the mound to warm up for the eighth inning.

"Look out, here comes Freddy," Nancy said, pointing down to the field. The Falcon mascot was prancing onto the grass, the fluffy blue and green feathers on his costume ruffling lightly in the soft breeze.

"I wonder what he's going to do," George said. "The last time I saw Freddy, he stole the umpire's hat and wouldn't give it back."

Freddy was now trotting comically toward the mound, lifting his clumsy bird feet high to keep from tripping. He had both hands in the air and his head tipped back as though running a victory lap after a race.

"It looks like he's after Showboat," Nancy said when the Falcon mascot stopped at the edge of the pitcher's mound. She grabbed her binoculars and focused on the mascot.

Freddy wrapped his feathery arms around the pitcher.

"He gave him something," Nancy said. The mascot released Sean and began to stride toward the sidelines. "A slip of yellow paper. I can see it in Sean's hand."

George strained to make out the paper, but without the aid of binoculars, she could only see the comical mascot hop away from the pitcher.

"Oh, no!" Nancy cried, gripping the binoculars tighter. She saw the anger in Sean's eyes and then saw him dash off the mound to tackle Freddy.

Blue and green feathers flew as the pitcher grabbed the mascot by the throat and the two of them rolled on the grass in front of nearly eight thousand spectators.

Chapter

Two

NANCY JUMPED to her feet as laughter rose from the crowd. Luke had tossed his catcher's mitt to the ground and run to where Sean and Freddy the Falcon were still rolling on the ground.

"It looks like Freddy got a little carried away," Nancy said as Luke pulled the pitcher off the mascot. "Sean is either very angry, or he's an awfully good actor."

"He *is* nicknamed Showboat," George said, smiling and standing beside Nancy.

The crowd continued to laugh as Freddy brushed himself off, thumbed his nose at Sean, and gleefully danced away. Sean was still struggling to break away from Luke. The pitcher's face was red with anger and his fists were clenched so hard his knuckles were white.

11

Nancy sank back into her seat, wondering if the whole show could have been planned.

When Freddy was finally off the field, Sean pulled free from his teammate and slowly took the mound again.

"Do you think they'll let him keep pitching after that?" Nancy asked.

"If it was just an act, they will," George said. "Besides, I don't even see the manager on the field."

George was right. Bill Barrows, the Falcons' manager, was the only person who could pull the pitcher from the game and he was nowhere to be seen.

"That's odd," George said. "Usually any manager is in the middle of everything."

Nancy watched the field, but Barrows didn't show up. On Luke's signal, Sean threw two more warm-up pitches and then shook his head when the umpire bellowed, "Play ball."

Nancy held her breath, hoping that Sean could get his concentration back, as the Ranger batter stepped up to the plate. Sean's first pitch was a fastball with no heat. The batter hit a line drive for a double and, on the next pitch, stole third.

The inning lasted for a good ten minutes. The Falcons managed to get two outs on grounders before another double brought in the tying run for the Rangers. George groaned.

The Falcons scored one more run in the bottom of the eighth to take the lead again, and

Nancy noted that Bill Barrows came out to give the scoring runner a high five as he crossed home plate. She wondered if the manager had been in the dugout the whole time.

"Does Barrows ever smile?" Nancy asked, noting his scowl as he turned back to the dugout.

"He's supposed to be incredibly serious about the game," George reported. "The sportswriters call him Mr. Baseball because he eats, breathes, and lives the sport. Nothing else seems to matter to him."

"I'd feel better if they put in a different pitcher," Nancy said as she watched Sean walk to the mound at the top of the ninth. The Falcons were just three outs from victory.

"I know what you mean," George agreed. "But maybe Sean will do better this inning."

Sean quickly walked two players. Two more flied out. The runners advanced, and now they were on second and third. The Falcons needed one more out. It should have been easy. Sean was facing the worst batter in the Rangers' lineup. The short, bulky player swung at the first two pitches and missed.

"One more strike and we win," George whispered. "And I bet it's going to be another fastball. This guy can't hit fastballs."

Instead, Sean threw a knuckleball. The pitch went wide, bouncing in the dirt and skittering into the wire mesh behind the batter's box. In a flurry of action Luke threw off his mask and dashed after the ball. George was instantly on her feet, and Nancy was beside her.

"Stop him! Stop him!" George yelled as the Ranger runner on third sprinted for home.

George's words were drowned out by cheers from the Ranger side of the field. The runner crossed the plate before Luke even got his hand on the ball. When the next batter hit a double, the Rangers scored again and took the lead.

From there on, things only got worse. When the Falcons finally came to bat in the bottom half of the ninth, they made two outs in a row. The next batter hit a high fly ball straight to the center fielder. When it was all over, the Rangers had won eight to seven.

Stormy Tarver screamed triumphantly and dashed up and down the stands shaking hands with her fans.

"I don't understand why Barrows didn't pull Sean out when he started pitching so badly," Nancy said.

"He may not have been able to," George explained. "Remember that Sean is here for a tune-up. Barrows might be under orders to play him a certain number of innings no matter what."

"Well, the day won't be a total loss," Nancy said, gathering up her things to leave. "We still get to have pizza with Luke."

"I just hope he's not in a bad mood," George replied as they headed down the ramp. They asked an usher how to get to the Falcon locker room. Following the man's directions, they walked down the hallway until they spotted a door marked No Entry. Nudging it open, Nancy saw that it led to a short set of steps ending at another door.

Once through the second doorway the girls found themselves in a long corridor. Nancy guessed that it provided access from the dugout to a parking lot exit for players and staff. She noticed several doors leading off the corridor, among them one labeled Locker Room.

The girls had come to a stop just outside it when a player charged out, nearly running Nancy over.

"Watch out!" George yelled as Nancy scrambled back against the wall. She did manage to get a look at the player's number as he flashed by. It was 52—Sean Reeves.

"Where's he going in such a hurry?" George asked indignantly.

"Do you suppose it has something to do with that note he got from Freddy?" Nancy said.

"Maybe," George replied. "Or he could just be running from Brenda."

Nancy saw that Brenda Carlton, the persistent and often annoying reporter for *Today's Times,* River Heights's tabloid newspaper, had stepped out of the locker room and was waving her reporter's notebook.

As Sean began to push his way through the

parking lot exit, Brenda yelled after him, "I'm going to get a story from you. One way or another."

"What story are you working on?" Nancy asked.

"The one about his being washed up," Brenda said to Nancy with a smile. "What else?"

"I don't think a slump means he's washed up," George said. "He'll be back in the majors soon, you just wait."

"I find that hard to believe after today's performance," Brenda said. "Anyway, what are you two doing here? In search of a mystery?"

"Hardly," Nancy answered. "We just came to see Luke."

"Who?" Brenda asked.

"I'm sure you don't remember him," George said.

"Try me," Brenda challenged.

"Luke Darlington," Nancy finally said. "We all went to high school with him."

Brenda shrugged. "I don't really remember him. He's the catcher, isn't he?"

"Right," George said, raising her chin slightly. "He played today."

"Yeah, but not too well," Brenda answered, rolling her eyes. With a quick wave over her shoulder, she headed off.

"She sure lost interest when she found out we were only meeting Luke," George said.

"Some people never change," Nancy said, grinning.

Several minutes later Bess appeared at the end of the corridor. "Am I late?" she asked.

"No," George said. "We'll probably have to wait awhile for Luke to finish changing."

"Did I miss Sean?" Bess asked.

Nancy and George laughed and nodded.

"I'm afraid so, Bess," Nancy said. "But after the way he pitched, I doubt he'd have been much fun."

"I heard from the fans at the concession stand that he wasn't doing too well," Bess said, removing her barrette to let her long hair fall loosely over her shoulders. "You'd never believe how much information you can get there."

"Like what?" George asked, folding her arms across her chest.

"Well, a lot of Ranger fans blame Stormy Tarver for the fact that the whole championship's being played in River Heights," Bess said. "They say Stormy could have avoided the accident at their stadium, but she was either too cheap or too broke to replace the pipe. She had been warned it was about to break."

"The fans certainly seemed to like her when she was in the stands," George remarked.

"It's kind of a love-hate thing, I guess," Bess said. "Ranger fans love her when she's winning and hate her when she's not. But I heard a lot of people talking about the fact that she's having financial problems."

Suddenly Nancy touched both her friends on the arm and motioned them to stop talking.

"Listen," she said. "I heard something, like someone groaning."

"I heard it, too," said Bess. "But where is it coming from?"

"This way," Nancy urged.

The moans got louder as they neared the door to the parking lot and silently pushed it open. George and Bess followed Nancy out into the bright sunlight. She checked right, then left, her eyes coming to rest on a large Dumpster pushed up against the outside wall of the stadium.

Slowly Nancy lifted the lid and boosted herself up to peek inside. Except for a little garbage, the bin was empty. But then the moaning sounded again.

Nancy peered around the back and saw a man lying in a heap in the narrow space between the Dumpster and the wall. His hands and feet were tied, his mouth gagged, and terror shone in his eyes!

Chapter

Three

THE MAN BEHIND the Dumpster was struggling against the ropes.

"Help me," Nancy said, turning back to George and Bess.

Together, the girls pushed the large metal bin out from the wall, then Nancy slid the handkerchief down from the man's mouth.

"Thank you," he gasped. "I didn't think I would ever be found."

"What happened?" Nancy asked as she worked at the knots in the ropes.

"I'm not sure," the man said excitedly. His black hair hung limply in his face, and his eyes were still wide with fear. "I left the field about halfway through the seventh inning. I was walking up the steps that lead from the corridor when I heard a noise behind me. Before I could turn around, someone hit me on the head and everything went black. The next thing I remember was waking up behind this Dumpster."

"Do you work at the Roost?" George asked, eyeing the man's plain blue jeans and green T-shirt.

"No, no," he said, pulling his hands free from the ropes. "I'm Anthony Reyes."

The three girls stared at him blankly.

"You know," he went on, "Freddy the Falcon."

Nancy's eyes grew round.

"You're the guy in the bird suit?" Bess said, surprised.

Anthony nodded, then reached down to untie the ropes that still held his feet.

Nancy frowned. "And you say you were hit over the head *before* the eighth inning?"

"That's right," Anthony replied.

"Then who was bugging Sean Reeves out on the mound?" George asked Nancy.

"I don't know, but it made Sean mad enough to tackle whoever was in that costume," Nancy said, raising her eyebrows. "I'm calling the police."

"There's a phone by the front entrance," Bess said. "I'll show you."

It took Nancy only a few minutes to report the mugging of Freddy the Falcon.

"The police are on their way," she told Anthony, whom she found walking stiffly up and down the hall. "Would you mind telling us why you were leaving before the end of the game?"

"I umpire youth baseball at five every Sunday," Reyes stated without hesitation. "If we're at home, I always leave before the last two innings to beat traffic and get there on time. The Falcons help sponsor the league, so they're happy to have me involved," Reyes said.

Dozens of people would have known about Anthony's schedule, Nancy realized. Just about anyone could have mugged him.

"Let's see if we can find the Freddy the Falcon costume," Nancy said to them all.

Anthony and the girls searched for the feathered uniform in the corridor that led past the locker rooms. Then they headed back up to the wide walkway where fans had recently been funneled out of the stands. About a hundred feet short of the main exit, Nancy heard a rattle and squeak. In another moment she saw two men in white overalls pushing a low cart topped by six garbage cans.

Anthony and the girls stepped out of the way as the men pushed their load past.

"Wait a minute!" Nancy shouted, reaching into one of the cans. She had noticed a blue feather poking up.

The two men stopped and watched in surprise as Nancy pulled out the Freddy the Falcon costume. "The imposter must have dumped it," Nancy said as Anthony Reyes took the costume and began examining it.

"Where did that garbage can come from?" Nancy asked the workers.

"This whole bunch came from the Ranger side of the field," answered the taller of the two men.

"Stormy Tarver's side," George commented.

"She was gone when Freddy the Falcon went to the pitcher's mound," Nancy said. "I remember her being gone until the eighth inning when the Rangers pulled ahead."

"Do you think Stormy would do such a horrible thing?" Bess asked as the men pushed their cart on down the corridor.

"Someone did. But why?" George said, shaking her head. "Nancy, I bet this has something to do with the note Freddy gave Sean Reeves."

"Could be," Nancy answered, carefully examining the corridor for more clues. "Maybe Luke will know something," she said as they returned to the locker room corridor.

As if on cue, Luke Darlington walked out of the locker room speaking with another player with mahogany-colored skin and short black hair. Without his uniform on, it took Nancy a minute to recognize him as the starting pitcher, Rod Sanders.

Luke smiled brightly at George and got a big grin from Bess when he remembered both her and Nancy's names. He introduced Rod, who greeted each of the girls.

"You played a good game," Sanders said, slapping Luke on the shoulder. "That run wasn't your fault. Reeves should have pitched what you called for." Reaching into his pocket, he added, "I'll see you later. I'm late."

As he pulled a set of car keys from his pocket, a piece of white paper fluttered to the ground. Nancy reached down and picked it up. It was blank except for the number *814* written on one side.

"Thanks," Rod said as she handed the note back to him. He quickly stuffed it into his pocket and walked toward the exit.

Nancy waited until Rod was out of sight, then put her hand on Luke's wrist.

"What did Rod mean when he said Sean should have thrown the pitch you asked for?" Nancy asked.

"In the ninth inning," Luke said with a shrug. "When the runner stole home, I asked for a fastball, but Luke threw a knuckleball instead. I wasn't ready for it—that's why it got away from me. It probably cost us the game."

"But I thought the pitcher was always supposed to throw what the catcher called for," Nancy said.

"He is," Luke answered, shaking his head. "Sean said he got the signals mixed up. It happens."

"Yes, I suppose," Nancy said quietly.

"Nancy thinks something strange is going on with Sean," George explained. "The mascot who hugged him in the eighth inning was an imposter, and he gave Sean a note." Then Nancy, George, and Bess told Luke all that had happened and asked him if he knew Anthony. The two men shook hands.

"This *is* strange," Luke said when they had finished. "Sean was upset, even before the game started. He snapped at me when I asked how his arm felt, and he didn't sign any autographs before the game like he usually does. It all seemed to start with a phone call he got just before we went on the field."

"He got a phone call?" Nancy asked.

Luke nodded. "He didn't say what it was about, but he was in a bad mood after it."

By the time the police arrived, Nancy was sure she had a mystery on her hands. She gave the officer a quick statement.

"I see you're still quite the detective," Luke said after listening to Nancy talk to the officers. "Why don't I take you to Sean's house. I'd like to make sure he's all right."

"Good idea," Nancy said. "As long as you don't mind bringing me back here later for my car."

Luke agreed. Nancy checked to make sure that Anthony was all right. Then she followed the catcher and her friends to the parking lot and climbed into Luke's sporty red sedan.

"Sean's a good guy and a great pitcher when he's on his game," Luke said as he turned into the street. "We've gotten to know each other some since he moved to River Heights."

"Is he in any kind of trouble?" Nancy asked from the backseat.

"Not that I know of," Luke replied as he turned into a subdivision of expensive new homes. "I don't think he has time to get into trouble. Every minute that he's not at the ball-park, he spends with his little girl."

"Sean has a daughter?" Bess asked, leaning forward in the seat beside Nancy.

"Yes, a five-year-old named Caitlin, who can already throw a mean fastball," Luke said, smiling a little. "Caitlin is the only thing more important to Sean than baseball."

"Is there a Mrs. Reeves?" Bess asked, peering at Luke curiously.

"No," Luke answered slowly. "Sean's wife died two years ago."

There was a moment of silence as Luke pulled his car up in front of a large new home with stained glass above the double front doors.

"Sean's renting this place," Luke said as he stopped the car.

"I guess it's true about all his money," George remarked, taking in the house.

"Yes, Sean's got a good contract," Luke said as they made their way to the door. "But he's going to have to get his game back if he wants to keep it."

Nancy surveyed the well-kept yard as Luke rang the doorbell. She was wondering what would make a seasoned professional tackle a mascot and then dash out of the stadium after the game.

Sean cracked the door open. He was still in his dirty, grass-stained uniform. Though he was over six feet tall, Nancy thought he looked more like a frightened child than a famous baseball player. His dark hair was tousled and his broad shoulders hunched forward. His deep brown eyes expressed a mixture of fear and suspicion.

"Luke," he said. The word sounded more like an accusation than a greeting. Rather than invite the group in, Sean stood in the doorway, blocking the entrance.

"We came over to see if everything was all right," Luke said. He was stammering a little, as though searching for words. "These are my friends, Nancy Drew, George Fayne, and Bess Marvin."

Sean's eyes moved cautiously from one to the other. But even when Bess flashed him her most flirtatious smile, Sean's expression remained glum. "I'm okay, but kind of busy," he said firmly. "See you tomorrow." He started to close the door.

"Wait," Luke said, holding the door open with his right hand. "Just let us come in and talk for a while, maybe have something to drink." Luke was calm but absolutely determined.

Nancy saw the tendons on the sides of Sean's neck stand out as he glared at Luke. For a moment Nancy was uncertain which man would win the stare-down.

"All right," Sean said, finally stepping away from the doorway.

Nancy, George, and Bess followed Luke into a spacious tiled entryway. To the left was a formal living room. On the right was the dining room, and through an arched doorway Nancy could see the kitchen.

"Have a seat. I'll bring some lemonade," Sean said, motioning to a couch.

"Please, let us help," Nancy said brightly.

Luke led the way to the kitchen. Sean brought up the rear, still looking as though he'd like to throw them all out.

As Luke and Sean fixed lemonade, Nancy took in the surroundings. The big kitchen had gleaming white countertops and all the latest appliances. A high counter formed one side of the kitchen area, and beyond it was a family room that looked as if it had been ransacked. An end table was overturned and magazines were scattered on the floor. A vase had been broken, jagged pieces of blue glass embedded in the carpet.

Nancy felt Bess's hand on her arm. She, too, had noticed the disarray.

"What happened?" Luke asked calmly. "It looks like there's been a fight."

Sean shrugged and glanced uneasily at the family room. "Caitlin just knocked over some things."

"Sean, Nancy is a detective. If you're in some kind of trouble, she can help," Luke said.

Sean's eyes narrowed. "I'm not in any trouble. Like I said, Caitlin just got a little rambunctious."

"We know about the mascot," Nancy broke in. "He was an imposter."

27

Sean's face turned red and his hands clenched into fists. "It was all an act," he said.

Nancy surveyed the room again, this time spotting a piece of slightly crumpled yellow paper by the telephone that sat on the counter. She walked casually around the counter and perched herself on the stool closest to the phone. Without touching the paper, she read the words scribbled in large block letters.

Nancy couldn't believe it! Lose the game or Caitlin dies, it said.

Chapter

Four

NANCY REACHED SLOWLY for the note and glanced up to see Sean's eyes riveted on her. She reread the words, convinced that they could mean only one thing. Sean's daughter had been kidnapped.

"Sean," she said gently. "If something has happened to Caitlin, you'll need help."

Sean followed behind Luke as he crossed the room to take the note from Nancy's hand.

Luke's expression was serious. "Nancy's right," he said to his friend.

Defeat crossed Sean's face. He settled onto a stool and, with his elbows propped on the counter, dropped his head to his hands.

"They said they'd hurt Caitlin if anyone found out," Sean said slowly. "I have to do what they say, it's the only way."

Luke went to Sean, putting his hands on the

pitcher's shoulders. "You have to tell us what's going on," he said. "Nancy's the best detective around. She can help you and she'll be careful."

"Sean," Nancy said firmly. "Where is Caitlin?"

"I don't know," the pitcher said at last, shaking his head. "I left her here with the sitter and everything was fine until—"

"Until what?" Nancy asked.

"Until just before the game," Sean said. He glanced toward George and Bess.

"It's okay," Nancy said. "They've helped me on lots of cases. We're a team."

Finally, with a deep sigh, Sean turned back to Nancy and Luke. "Until just before the game," he said. "The manager called me into his office. He said I had a phone call. It was Rebecca, the sitter, and she was hysterical. She kept saying, 'They're going to hurt us.'" Sean paused and rubbed his palm across his forehead.

"Take it easy," Nancy said, touching Sean's arm.

Sean took a deep breath and closed his eyes for a minute as though concentrating. "She said, 'Do exactly what I say, or they're going to hurt Caitlin. They want you to stay in the game and wait for instructions, but don't tell anyone about this, or you'll be sorry.' She was sobbing, and then the phone went dead."

"Just before the eighth inning, the mascot gave you this note," Nancy said, pointing to the piece of yellow paper.

Sean nodded. He got up from the stool and paced across the room.

"But it wasn't the real mascot," Bess said.

"Just someone who stole the mascot costume," Nancy added.

"Do you have any idea who could have done this?" George asked.

"No," Sean said firmly, turning toward them. "I can think of lots of people who'd want the Falcons to lose the game, but nobody would take my little girl—nobody is that cruel."

"Someone is," Nancy said gravely. "And we need to find out who." She hopped down from her stool and paced the floor near the counter. "After you got the phone call, did anyone besides the fake mascot contact you or talk to you about Caitlin?" Nancy asked, stopping in front of the large window that framed Sean's backyard.

"No one," Sean said. He shook his head slowly as he walked to the coffee table in the family room, picking up a framed picture.

"Is that Caitlin?" Nancy asked gently.

Sean nodded and handed her the picture. It showed a smiling five-year-old with dark hair cropped short around her face and big brown eyes that immediately reminded Nancy of Sean. She was wearing a baseball hat with the logo of Sean's major league team, the Captains.

"She's cute," Nancy said, wondering where Caitlin was and if her sparkling eyes were now filled with fear. She noticed Sean staring at the wall and guessed that he was fighting back tears.

"We'll find her," Nancy said. She passed the picture across the counter to George and Bess.

Luke crossed the room and put his hand back on Sean's shoulder. "Nancy's right. We'll find Caitlin." He steered Sean to the stool by the counter.

"Is this the way the house looked when you came home?" Nancy asked.

Sean nodded.

"What do you know about your baby-sitter?" Nancy pressed. She had walked around to the kitchen side of the counter to stand beside Bess and George. She faced Sean, trying to hold his attention.

"Her name is Rebecca Carter. Caitlin likes her, and I was lucky to find her on such short notice," Sean said. "I got to River Heights a few days before the play-offs and had to find someone to stay with Caitlin right away. Rebecca sat for Caitlin last night, during the first game. Her address and phone number are there in the book." He pointed to a small green address book by the phone.

Nancy reached for it and began flipping through the pages. "How did you find her?" she asked.

"Rod told me about her," Sean said. He had begun to tap his fingers on the counter. "She baby-sat for him earlier in the season."

Nancy looked at Luke.

"Rod Sanders," he said. "The pitcher I was talking to after the game today."

Nancy turned back to the address book, where she found Rebecca's address. Pulling a small notebook and pen from the back pocket of her jeans, Nancy wrote down 4018 Oak St., G-7, and then the phone number.

"She lives in an apartment?" Nancy asked, putting the pad and pen back in her pocket.

"That's right." Sean got up from his stool and began to pace again. "I don't know where, exactly, because she drove here on her own. But she did say she might have to move out if she couldn't catch up on her rent payments."

"She doesn't have another job?" Nancy asked, closing Sean's address book.

"Not as far as I know," Sean said. "I told her someone her age ought to be in school. She just laughed and said she didn't have enough money."

"How old is she?" Nancy asked, wishing she had a photo of the sitter.

"I don't know," Sean said, shrugging. "Nineteen or twenty, I'd guess. She has red hair and is a little taller than you, I think."

"What does her car look like?" Nancy asked.

"It's a beat-up green sedan. She parked it in the driveway this morning. Now it's gone," Sean said, raising his hands to show his confusion.

"Why would the kidnapper take Rebecca's car?" George asked.

"I don't know," Nancy said. "Was any other room in the house ransacked?"

"Yes," Sean replied, and this time his voice

was tinged with anger. "They were in Caitlin's room."

Sean led Nancy down a hall and stopped by the doorway to a bedroom. The white walls were decorated with posters of cartoon characters, and a pile of soft stuffed animals covered one corner of the bed across the room from a sunny window.

Nancy saw muddy tracks that led from the window across the light-colored carpet to Caitlin's bed. The white, ruffled bedspread had been pulled partly off the bed, and some of the stuffed animals were on the floor.

"It looks like someone came in the window to grab Caitlin," George said, peeking over Nancy's shoulder.

"Does Caitlin still take naps?" Nancy asked.

"Sometimes," Sean said. "After lunch, from about twelve-thirty to one-thirty. I left early— about eleven. I had some errands to do. And I needed some time alone before the game."

"So the kidnapping could have happened during Caitlin's nap," Bess suggested.

"But why would anyone go into the family room when they had already kidnapped Caitlin from the bedroom?" Luke asked.

"Maybe Rebecca heard them," Nancy said. Images flashed through Nancy's mind of the baby-sitter overhearing the kidnappers and not knowing what to do. She walked to the window and leaned out. She could see large, smudged footprints in the flower bed beneath the window.

The screen had been removed and laid against the side of the house.

Nancy turned and followed the muddy tracks. They began to fade after the intruder had turned from the bed. A faint trail made a path to the door, but Nancy could not determine if the kidnapper had left the bedroom or not. He could have gone down the hall to the family room where he struggled with a desperate Rebecca. Or perhaps Rebecca had helped with the plot. It was possible that she and the kidnapper had ransacked the family room to make it look as if there'd been a struggle. At any rate, Rebecca and her car were gone, a fact that puzzled Nancy.

"Bess and I will go outside, and the rest of you start checking inside," Nancy said, starting back down the hall toward the family room. "Try not to touch anything. Just look for clues."

Nancy and Bess went through the family room and out the back door. The fenced yard was edged by flower beds. Nancy walked carefully to Caitlin's bedroom window. The smeared tracks disappeared in the lush green grass about two feet from it.

"We need to check the gates in the fence," Nancy said.

"I'll go this way," Bess offered, pointing to her right.

"Great," Nancy said. "I'll look by the garage."

She found nothing out of place along the back of the house or along the fence. A gate by the garage was closed and latched. Nancy opened it and went through. She kept her eyes on the ground as she walked beside the garage. On her right a row of large shrubs separated the side yard from a narrow alley. Nancy checked the shrubs carefully for any bits of fabric or paper, but found nothing.

Two concrete steps led to the side door of the garage. Nancy saw some small pieces of gray clay on the top step. It was different from the mud at the back of the house. She was about to turn away when she caught sight of a piece of white paper in the marigold bed near the step. It looked as if it might have come from a small notepad. When Nancy picked it up and turned it over, she saw what seemed to be a shopping list. Milk, chips, Yummy Bunnies, and clothesline were listed.

"I didn't find anything," Bess said from behind Nancy. "There's another gate on the far side of the house, but it's closed."

"This one was closed, too," Nancy said as she turned around with the list. "But this could be a clue."

Before Bess could take the list, Nancy heard yelling from inside the house, and George came running out to the gate.

"Nancy! You'd better come quick," she said tensely. She pivoted and disappeared back into the house. Nancy and Bess quickly followed.

As they rushed in through the back door, Nancy saw a well-dressed man and woman in their fifties standing in the ransacked family room.

"She can't be gone!" the woman blurted out.

"She *is* gone," the man said angrily, turning to the woman. "We should have expected it."

Sean stood just a few feet away from the couple, his eyes reflecting his anger. Luke was at his side, his hands raised slightly as though ready for a fight.

Nancy stopped just inside the door. It was clear to her that Sean was very near the breaking point.

"We should have known he'd let something happen to our granddaughter," the gray-haired man continued, raising his finger and shaking it in Sean's face. "It's all your fault!"

Sean knocked the man's hand away and took a step closer, so that he towered over the older man. "I think you'd better leave," he said.

"I'll leave after I've made you pay," the other man growled back. He took a step backward and launched his fist at Sean's face.

Bess gasped as Sean raised his left arm to ward off the attack and then, reflexively, pulled his right arm back, ready to strike a blow of his own.

Chapter

Five

"Sean, NO!" Nancy yelled as the pitcher raised his fist. She lunged between him and the gray-haired man, Luke right beside her.

"That's not going to help get Caitlin back," she said firmly.

"Nancy's right," Luke agreed. "You can't help Caitlin if you're in jail."

Sean relaxed slightly. He took a step backward, nearly bumping into the coffee table.

"These are Caitlin's grandparents," George offered, breaking the tense silence. "I was introduced to them while you were outside."

The man pulled on the lapels of his sport coat and nodded a brisk greeting to Nancy. "And who are you?" he demanded.

"This is Nancy Drew," Luke said, stepping between them. "The best de—"

"A best friend of Luke's from school," Nancy

cut in quickly. She stepped across the room and offered to shake hands.

"Bert Zabowski," the man said gruffly. "And this is my wife, Stella. We came down to River Heights to surprise Caitlin, and then we found out she was gone. . . ." He shook his head and added, "I suppose you know what trouble my son-in-law has caused."

"What do you mean?" Nancy asked seriously. "Sean hasn't done anything wrong."

"I have to disagree with that," Bert said. "His involvement in sports is the reason Caitlin has disappeared."

"But, Mr. Zabowski," George said, "you can't blame Sean for Caitlin's kidnapping just because he's a baseball player. It's not his fault."

"But it *is* his fault," Bert said, raising both hands. "It's his fault he's pitching baseballs instead of working in my electronics firm."

"And it's his fault that Caitlin was in this horrible little town," Stella added, her voice strained. "He should have let us take her back to Chicago for the summer."

"Please, Mr. and Mrs. Zabowski," Nancy said, "we need to concentrate our efforts on getting Caitlin back."

"We need to call the police," Bert bellowed.

"Of course," Nancy said calmly. "But let Sean handle that. He *is* Caitlin's father. The rest of us need to keep this absolutely secret."

Bert fumed silently for a moment, then shook his finger at Sean. "You'd better not fail," he said, then turned to Stella, who had begun crying quietly. Bert put his arm around her and led her toward the front door.

"It's hard to tell which side they're on," Bess said when they were gone.

"They never liked me," Sean said, shoving his hands into his pockets. "And they hate baseball."

"They wanted Caitlin to live with them?" Nancy asked.

"That's right," Sean said, pacing across the floor. He turned away from the wrecked family room and looked through the window at the tranquil backyard. "They think they're better parents than I am. For the past year they've been on a campaign to convince me of that."

"Could they want Caitlin bad enough to take her?" Nancy asked.

"They wouldn't take her and show up back here," Sean said after a moment. "And besides, I can't picture either of them in Freddy's costume."

"He's got a point there," Bess said with a hint of sarcasm as she settled herself on the couch.

"And even if they took Caitlin, they wouldn't care about the outcome of the game," George added.

"Unless they were just trying to throw us off the trail," Nancy said, then sighed. "Still, I suppose you're right, they're not very likely suspects. But let's not count them out completely."

"So what next?" Sean asked.

"First I want you to take a look at this," Nancy

said, pulling the shopping list from her pocket. "Do you recognize it?"

Sean took the list and examined it carefully. "Yummy Bunnies are Caitlin's favorite snack," he said.

"You mean those little cookies that are shaped like rabbits?" Bess asked. "The ones that come in all different colors?"

"That's right," Sean said, handing the note back to Nancy. "Caitlin eats them by the boxful."

"What about the handwriting?" Nancy asked. "Is it yours, or Rebecca's?"

Sean shook his head. "I didn't write this list, and I don't know what Rebecca's handwriting looks like."

Nancy went to the counter and compared the list to the note Sean had received during the game, but the writing didn't match. "I know it's going to be hard for you to do, Sean, but we really have to call the police."

"No police!" Sean whirled on Nancy. "Luke said you'd be careful."

"I will, but I want to help you get your little girl back," Nancy said gently. "Calling the police is the best way to do that. I know the chief."

"What can he do?" Sean asked, raising his hands in the air in a gesture of helplessness. "Except bring the press down on us like flies. They'll get wind of this and won't let go until it's on the front page of every newspaper in the country. And then what will happen to Caitlin?"

Nancy remembered Brenda chasing Sean down the corridor and sighed. "Chief McGinnis will know how to deal with this," she said firmly.

"She's right," Luke said.

Sean picked up the picture of Caitlin again and stared at it for a second. "All right," he said at last. "But if you're wrong, if the newspapers find out and Caitlin ends up——"

"We'll be careful," Nancy cut in gently, moving toward the telephone.

Nancy had to look up Chief McGinnis's home telephone number in the phone book. She wasn't going to trust anyone with this case except the chief himself. The phone rang three times before Mrs. McGinnis answered. After introducing herself, Nancy learned that the chief was out but was due back in half an hour.

"He's not there," she said, hanging up the telephone. "Luke, why don't you take us back to the stadium so I can get my car. I'll call again from there. Sean, meet us there in about thirty minutes. And bring the note and the shopping list. The chief will want to see them."

Sean nodded and walked to the door as Nancy, Bess, George, and Luke headed for the car.

"Back again?"

Nancy couldn't mistake that voice—it was Brenda Carlton's. She was still carrying her notebook as she crossed the parking lot near the players' entrance to the stadium.

"Did you get your story?" Nancy asked, forcing a smile.

"Not from Sean," she said. "But I got some other interviews. How about you?" Brenda cocked her head to one side in a way that told Nancy she was fishing for information. "Have you found out anything interesting?"

"As I told you before," Nancy said, shrugging her shoulders, "we just came to see an old friend."

Brenda eyed her suspiciously. "I'm going to be watching you, Nancy Drew," she said. "And if you *have* found a mystery at the Roost, I'll figure out what it is."

"You'll be wasting your time," Nancy said casually. But as she walked after Luke, Bess, and George, all of Sean's words came flooding back to her.

"Brenda is going to be a problem," Nancy whispered as she caught up with her friends.

Luke had left his wallet in the locker room and wanted to pick it up. After he got it, he and Nancy dashed up to the pay phone at the main ticket office. Bess and George decided to wait, sitting on a couple of chairs in the corridor outside the locker room. It had been nearly two hours since the game ended, and even the celebrating Rangers had left the stadium.

Chief McGinnis answered, and Nancy explained as briefly as she could about the kidnapping. She told him that she and Sean would meet him in the parking garage of the River Heights Mall in half an hour. She thought it best to let Sean drive, since it would look less suspicious if the kidnappers were tailing him. She got a description of the pitcher's forest green sports car from Luke and relayed it to Chief McGinnis.

Just as she and Luke were returning for George and Bess, Sean appeared. He had changed into faded jeans and a light blue T-shirt that set off his dark hair and eyes.

"You're just in time," Nancy said. "We're all set to meet Chief McGinnis in the parking garage at the mall. If anyone is following you, it'll just look like we have to pick up something. I doubt that a tail will follow us into a parking garage. It would be too easy to get caught."

Sean stopped and nervously checked the exit at the end of the corridor. "Do you think I'm being followed?"

"We can't be too careful," Nancy said, shaking her head. "Now let's go. I'll ride with you."

Before they got away, a heavy, balding man in designer sweats stepped out of the locker room. He was at least two inches shorter than Sean and had a small birthmark that looked a bit like a smudge of dirt on his right cheek. Nancy recognized him as Bill Barrows, the Falcons' manager.

Surprise flashed across Barrows's face when he saw Sean, Luke, and the girls, but then he smiled. He was chewing a large wad of gum.

"I figured you'd be gone by now," he said firmly. "You have another game tomorrow, and

I'd like to see you pitch better than you did today."

Sean began to clench and unclench his fists nervously. "I'm on my way home now," he lied.

"Well, at least you're with fans," Barrows said, focusing on the feathered Falcon pins that Nancy and George still wore.

Nancy noticed that Barrows had one of the same pins on his shirt.

"Get some rest," Barrows added before heading for another door along the corridor.

Watching him leave, Nancy caught sight of a small blue feather on the shoulder of his sweatshirt. She guessed it was from the badge he wore, but she couldn't help thinking of the feathered mascot costume.

"When did Barrows get to the stadium today?" Nancy whispered to Sean.

"He was here when I arrived," Sean said. "That was about twelve-thirty."

Nancy ran the timing over in her mind. If Caitlin was taken during her nap, the kidnapping would have occurred between twelve-thirty and one-thirty. Sean had gotten the call from Rebecca before the players had gone out to the field. It didn't sound as if Barrows could have been involved.

"Barrows has been with the Falcons a long time, hasn't he?" George asked the players.

"Yes, and he practically lives at the stadium," Luke said as the group left the stadium and walked across the lot. "I don't think he has much of a life outside of baseball. He's pretty close to retirement. It's kind of sad."

Luke offered to give George and Bess rides home.

"That would be great," George said, and Nancy saw the sparkle in her eye.

"You have to let us know what happens," Bess said. George and Luke both nodded in agreement. "And if there's anything we can do to help get Caitlin back."

"Of course," Nancy said, glancing at her watch. "Why don't we try for breakfast together since we didn't get pizza tonight? We can meet at the Gilded Cage, say at nine-thirty?"

Her friends agreed, and Bess gave Nancy a knowing look as George walked to Luke's car. Luke held the front door for George so she could sit beside him.

"Why don't I drive your Mustang home?" she whispered to Nancy. "I really think George and Luke would like to be alone."

Nancy grinned. "You're right," she said, handing over her keys to Bess.

Nancy followed Sean to his car. Soon they were headed down the street, through the intersection where she had the close call that morning, toward the mall. Nancy checked behind them, but saw no one following.

When they reached the parking garage at the mall, Sean lowered his window and took a ticket from the attendant.

"McGinnis said he'd find us," Nancy said as Sean started up the ramp.

They cruised slowly up the various levels of the garage. Nancy was looking carefully for the familiar face of the chief when she heard the squeal of tires in front of her.

"Look out!" she cried.

A battered blue sedan was backing out from its parking space directly in front of them. Sean slammed on his brakes, barely avoiding a collision.

The car stopped and a dirty, bearded man emerged from the passenger side of the vehicle. He started toward them. As he rounded the sedan, his camouflage jacket opened a few inches. Nancy saw the leather strap that she knew was part of a shoulder holster.

"Watch it," she said tensely. "He's got a gun."

Chapter

Six

Sean cautiously rolled down his window. "I'm a friend," the man with the gun said as he leaned on the edge of the open window. "Mc-Ginnis sent me."

Nancy relaxed slightly and noticed that the man's clothes were dirty and ragged, and he wasn't much taller than she was. He had dark eyes and skin and acted calm and businesslike.

"There's an empty parking space on your right," he said, his voice low. "Park there." He raised himself up from the side of the car and motioned to his partner in the beatup sedan.

Sean glanced at Nancy, his eyes questioning her.

"Do what he says," Nancy advised.

As Sean pulled forward and into the empty parking spot, she saw Chief McGinnis behind the wheel of an unmarked car beside them.

The stranger had already climbed into the backseat of McGinnis's car. His partner had pulled the battered sedan into the spot on the opposite side of Sean's car. The chief motioned for Nancy and Sean to join him.

"Meet Chief McGinnis," Nancy said as Sean got into the front seat and she slid into the back. Sean nodded.

"This is Victor Delgado," McGinnis said, motioning toward the backseat. He was watching Sean carefully. "Victor is in charge of the area office of the FBI."

Nancy felt a chill run through her. She had thought of the FBI but hadn't expected McGinnis to call them without consulting her or Sean. She was watching Sean as his hand came down with a slap on the padded dash of the car.

"You promised this would be kept quiet," he said fiercely to Nancy. "Now the FBI is in on it. Maybe we should just write a press release!"

"I've been doing this for ten years, and I haven't been burned by the press yet," Victor said, his voice firm with authority. "When you say FBI to the press, they start looking for men in three-piece suits. They'll never know we're here."

"We," Sean muttered in exasperation. "How many FBI agents are in on this?"

"We'll call in as many people as we need to do the job," Victor said patiently.

For the second time that day, Nancy saw Sean's anger rise toward the boiling point.

"It's okay," McGinnis said reassuringly. "The

FBI is the best agency to handle a kidnapping. They have the experience and the technology, and they can work fast. Besides . . ." His voice trailed off and his gaze shifted away for a moment before he faced Sean again and continued. "I had to notify them."

"The Lindbergh Law," Nancy said quietly. She had heard about it from her father, the well-known attorney Carson Drew. It had been passed after the kidnapping of the small son of a famous pilot, Charles Lindbergh. "It says the FBI can take over any kidnapping case after twenty-four hours."

"The girl knows her law," Victor said evenly.

Sean sank back into his seat with a sigh. "All right," he said at last. "But promise you won't let the press get a hold of this."

"You got it," Victor said. "Now tell us everything."

He and McGinnis listened as Nancy and Sean relayed the day's events and handed over the note and list. When they had finished, Victor leaned back in his seat and looked out the car window as though deep in thought.

"There has been no ransom demand?" Delgado asked Sean.

Sean shook his head.

"No telephone calls after the first one? No instructions, except to lose the game?" Victor pressed.

In answer to each question, Sean shook his head slowly.

"The kidnappers may be taking their time, or there may not be a ransom request," Victor said. "If that's the case, we're going to have to catch these guys some other way."

"Most kidnappers are captured when they try to pick up the ransom money," Chief McGinnis explained. "There are all sorts of ways to set traps."

"So we're at a dead end?" Sean asked helplessly.

"No," said Victor. "It's just going to be harder."

"You'll want to go through his house," Nancy said. "There may be prints there."

"Yes," said Victor with a nod. "But the kidnappers could be watching the house and might have already tapped the phone. We don't want to tip them off that we're involved."

"How about a disguise?" Nancy asked.

Victor's eyes flashed at Nancy. "That's exactly what we'll do."

He handed Sean a card with a phone number written on it. "When you get home tonight, call this number and ask for emergency plumbing service. Say you have a broken pipe. If the kidnappers are listening in or watching, they won't know that the plumbers are really agents. My men will check your house for fingerprints and install a recorder on your phone. We'll sneak one in, and he'll stay and watch the house and monitor the machine while you're away."

"You're treating this like it's the work of professionals," Nancy said grimly.

Victor paused a moment. "It could be just about anybody—including professionals," he said. "That means we have to be extra careful."

Nancy thought about her first call to McGinnis from Sean's house. She was glad he hadn't been home.

"My office will be working with the FBI on this," McGinnis said. "But you won't see any of our officers either. Everybody will be in plain clothes."

"We'll see what we can find out from people in the neighborhood, but it won't be easy because we'll have to do it without letting on that there's been a kidnapping. It's mostly a matter of watching, listening, and waiting for the kidnappers to make another move," Victor said to Sean. "You'll have to be patient."

"Catching the kidnappers will be secondary to getting Caitlin back," McGinnis broke in. "We won't do anything to put her in more danger without consulting you, even if it means letting the kidnappers get away."

Sean let out a long breath. "What if they ask me to throw another game?"

"I can't tell you what to do there," Victor said. "That'll be up to you."

Sean's frustration boiled over. "Okay, Mr. FBI," Sean said, raising his voice. "If it were your kid and you were pitching, what would you do?"

Victor's expression didn't change as he answered, "I'd throw the game."

Sean's shoulders sagged in defeat. "What if I get another phone call?" he asked at last.

"Well, if we're lucky, it will come to your house and we can trace it," Victor said reassuringly. "We can't put recorders on the phones at the ballpark without tipping off management to the kidnapping. So if you get another call there, try to remember everything you can about what's said and any background sounds. Report it immediately to the agent staying at your house, or call the police with the information."

Sean nodded, acting somewhat reassured.

"What about the note and the shopping list?" Nancy asked.

"We'll check them out," he said. "From what you've told me, I'd guess Rebecca was taken along with Caitlin. But it's possible she helped with the kidnapping. We'll see what we can find out about her."

"Clothesline is one of the items on the list," Nancy began. "If the list was dropped by the kidnappers, they could have used the line to tie the victims up."

"You have sharp eyes, Nancy Drew," Victor said, leaning back against the car seat. "But you can relax now. We won't need you anymore."

Nancy was about to protest when McGinnis came to her defense. "Nancy's no novice. She's helped me on a lot of cases," he said. "In fact, just a couple months ago she solved a murder up at the Riverfront Amusement Park."

Nancy saw Victor's mouth open, but before he could speak, Sean jumped in.

"You said you'd consult me," he said firmly. "I say Nancy's in."

Delgado's mouth closed and he let out a sigh. "All right," he said.

"I don't like that guy," Sean said when he and Nancy were back in his car. "He scares me, even though he does act like he cares about Caitlin."

Nancy shared Sean's feelings, though she was reluctant to say so. "But McGinnis seems to trust him, so he must be good."

"Yeah, I know," Sean said as he steered his sports car out of the parking garage and toward Nancy's house. "I keep thinking that this is just a bad dream, that when I get home, Caitlin will be there."

"We all wish it would happen that way." Nancy glanced at Sean and was struck once again by his deep brown eyes and how much Caitlin's were like his. She desperately hoped she'd see the two of them together someday.

When Sean pulled up in front of Nancy's house, she opened the passenger door and started to get out.

"When will I see you again?" Sean asked.

"Tomorrow," Nancy promised. "I'll figure out a way to get in touch with you, maybe through

Luke. Try to get some rest. I know it'll be hard, but you'll need it."

Nancy walked toward the lighted front porch. Her Mustang was in the driveway, where Bess had left it. She unlocked the front door and found the house dark except for the entry and hall lights. Her father and the housekeeper, Hannah Gruen, had already gone to their rooms. Though she'd missed dinner, Nancy found she wasn't hungry. The kidnapping had ruined her appetite.

But she *was* exhausted. Up in her bedroom she'd barely pulled on her nightgown when she dropped onto her bed and fell asleep.

The sun had already warmed the sidewalk when Nancy left her house the next morning on her way to the Gilded Cage restaurant. She was just reaching for the door handle on her Mustang when a sleek, black sedan pulled up and parked behind her. Nancy's hand dropped away from the car door as she watched an attractive woman step out of the car. Her short hair was carefully styled and almost as dark as the black skirt and jacket she wore.

"Excuse me," she said as she closed the car door. "Are you Nancy Drew?"

"Yes," Nancy said somewhat cautiously.

"Madeline de Grasse," the woman announced as she handed Nancy her business card.

Nancy glanced at the card, her curiosity piqued. Attorney at Law, it said under the name.

"I understand you were at the residence of Sean Reeves yesterday evening," the attorney probed.

Nancy was instantly wary. "Do you have some interest in Mr. Reeves?" she asked.

The woman studied Nancy. "Some time ago I was retained by Bert and Stella Zabowski," she said tersely. "They called me early this morning with new information, which compelled me to get right on the case."

Nancy struggled to avoid showing the shock she felt when she heard the names of Caitlin's grandparents.

"I need to talk to you about Mr. Reeves's inability to care for his daughter," Ms. de Grasse said.

"I don't know what you mean," Nancy said. She felt her back stiffen.

"I mean his failure as a father," Ms. de Grasse went on. "The Zabowskis feel that the girl's disappearance proves he is an unfit parent. They have asked me to file a petition with the court requesting custody of the child."

Chapter

Seven

Nancy's mind reeled. "When will a petition be filed?" she asked. She knew that reporters would jump on a custody battle involving a well-known pitcher. And if the petition included mention of Caitlin's disappearance, Sean's secret would be out.

"As soon I have enough information," Ms. de Grasse said. "The Zabowskis feel that the sooner they get Caitlin away from her father, the better it will be for the child."

Nancy fought back an urge to beg the woman to wait, to remind her of how much danger it would put Caitlin in if word of her kidnapping was made public. She feared such an approach might play into the attorney's hands.

"I don't know what you're talking about," Nancy said. "And now, if you'll excuse me, I have to go."

The attorney raised her hand as though ready to make a point. Nancy reached for her car door and swung it open quickly. She was in the car with the door closed again before Ms. de Grasse could speak.

Nancy smiled broadly through the window at the flabbergasted attorney. She started the engine and waited, watching Ms. de Grasse frown and go back to her car. When she pulled out, Nancy followed her down the drive. Fortunately, the attorney wasn't the persistent type, she thought.

Five minutes later she was turning into the lot at the Gilded Cage, a favorite hangout for River Heights sports fans.

Inside, to the right of the doors, was a batting cage. A gold-painted backstop stood behind a home plate, facing a pitching machine. The whole thing was surrounded by heavy netting. Here diners sometimes got to watch Falcon players hit a few balls.

Nancy surveyed the half-full restaurant and walked to the front counter. "I'm here to meet some friends," Nancy told the hostess, and was directed to a booth in the back corner of the restaurant.

George smiled brightly at Nancy. She was sitting beside Luke, and Nancy couldn't help noticing that the two made a great-looking couple. His arm was draped casually across the seat behind George.

"Tell us what McGinnis said," Bess urged as Nancy slid into the booth beside her.

Nancy told her friends about the meeting with Victor Delgado and about Madeline de Grasse. She stopped only once when a waitress came to take their order.

"I knew the Zabowskis would be trouble," Luke said tensely.

"If those court papers get filed, the press will find out about the kidnapping for sure," Nancy replied.

"I can't help but wonder whether the Zabowskis could be the kidnappers," George said after the waitress delivered their food. "Caitlin's disappearance seems too convenient. It gives them a perfect reason to try to take her away from her dad."

"I know," Nancy said. "And that could explain why they're not worried about anyone finding out she's gone."

"It's just hard to believe they'd kidnap their own granddaughter," Bess said, breaking off a piece of a huge cinnamon roll.

"True," Nancy answered. "Still, we have to consider them suspects."

"Right now they're about the only suspects," George said, spreading strawberry jam on an English muffin.

"What about Stormy Tarver?" Bess said. "If she really is broke, winning the series could be especially important. Besides, who cares more about the Rangers winning than their owner?"

"I agree," said Nancy. "I'm going to have to find out more about Stormy. The rumor that she's having financial problems is not much to go on."

"All right," said George. "Who else?"

Nancy paused for a minute before answering. "Rebecca," she said simply.

"But wasn't she kidnapped?" Bess asked.

"It looks like it," Nancy said, cocking her head to one side. "But looks can be deceiving."

"You mean Rebecca could have kidnapped Caitlin and then made it look like someone else was involved?" Luke asked.

"I think someone else *was* involved," Nancy said. "Even though the tracks outside Caitlin's window were smeared, they seemed to be too large to be a woman's, and they seemed to stop at the doorway to Caitlin's room. Maybe they just petered out there. Or maybe someone trashed the family room to make it look like there had been a struggle."

"Someone like Rebecca," George said, brushing Luke's arm as she leaned back in the booth.

"Could be," Nancy said, and pushed her empty plate to one side. "Whatever role Rebecca played in the kidnapping, we know she's important to the case. Then there's Bill Barrows."

"Is he a suspect?" George said in quiet surprise.

"Well," Nancy said, lacing her fingers together thoughtfully. "I remember looking for him after Sean tackled the mascot. He wasn't on the field. And when we saw him at the park last night, there was a blue feather on his shirt."

"But he was wearing a Falcon button," George replied. "The feather could have been from that."

"Besides," Bess added, "he would be the last person to ask Sean to throw a game, wouldn't he?"

Nancy was watching Luke. She had never thought of him as good-looking in high school, but that description definitely fit him now.

"Barrows would do anything to win," Luke said. "There's no way he'd make Sean throw a game. It just doesn't make sense."

"I guess not," Nancy said with a sigh. "But I want you to keep an eye on him, Luke."

"No problem," Luke said with a grin. "We tend to hang out together a lot these days."

Nancy laughed lightly. With three more games scheduled that week, Luke would be seeing his manager every day.

"What now?" Bess asked as Nancy slid out of the booth.

"I'd like to learn more about Stormy Tarver," Nancy said, leading the way to the cash register.

"We could stop at the library," George offered. "I remember an article about her in *Profiles* magazine, and I'm sure the library will have it."

"Good idea," Nancy said as the group left the restaurant. "I'll meet you there."

"I'll ride with you," Bess volunteered, raising an eyebrow at Luke and George for Nancy's benefit.

Nancy laughed and unlocked the doors of her

Mustang. She maneuvered her car through downtown River Heights, stopping at the stately two-story brick building that housed the city library. George and Luke met them on the front steps. Then they entered the large reading room lined with racks of magazines and newspapers.

George located *Profiles* and the article that had run earlier that summer. Nancy took the magazine and began to read out loud. "'Rangers owner Stormy Tarver said she was joking when she offered umpire Jack Middleman $1,000 to call strikes for her pitchers last week. But Middleman wasn't laughing when he reported the incident to the league office. He said Tarver stopped him in a dark parking lot outside a restaurant and offered him cash to call the game in the Rangers' favor.'"

Bess raised her eyebrows as Nancy read. She, George, and Luke were leaning over the table in rapt silence.

Nancy read on. "'Middleman didn't take the money. "The guy can't take a joke," said Tarver. "I was just trying to make the point that I didn't like his calls the week before." League officials are investigating, but no one really expects them to discipline Tarver. Given her track record for bizarre behavior, this could just be another publicity stunt.'"

"That sounds like Stormy," Luke said. "She's a real case."

"There's more," Nancy said, scanning the page. "Listen to this. 'Some people think that

Tarver might have been serious, though. After all, this is the same woman who once poured laxative into the opposing team's juice jug to try to help the Rangers out of a losing situation.'"

All four laughed, but then Bess asked, "Do you think Stormy would try to get rid of Sean just to win the series?"

"It's possible," Nancy said. She silently began to scan the rest of the story.

"Let's see what else we can find," George said to Luke. They got up and went back to the magazine racks, returning after several minutes with an issue of *Play Ball* magazine.

"Here's a profile of the Falcons done at the start of the season," George said, handing the magazine to Nancy.

The article predicted the team would play second fiddle to the Rangers. Next, it gave short profiles on several Falcon players.

"There are a lot of names here I don't recognize," Nancy said, skimming the article.

"There's a big turnover in the minors," Luke said across the table from Nancy. "If a guy plays really well, he gets moved up to the majors, and if he plays really badly, he's moved down to an AA team."

"Here's a picture of Rod Sanders," Nancy said. "The caption says he's twenty-nine and has been in River Heights for five years."

Nancy noticed the faraway, almost sad expression in Luke's eyes.

"He's getting old," Luke explained. "Anyone

who hasn't made it to the majors by the time he's thirty should start looking for another job."

"I wonder how Rod feels about Sean joining the Falcons?" Nancy asked, flipping to another page.

"He bashed his locker with a baseball bat when he heard about it," Luke said, frowning. "And when Sean got so much press for winning the first game, Rod was really down."

"He shouldn't be so jealous," Bess said.

"Maybe, but this isn't just some school-yard game," Luke said, his voice rising slightly. "It's his career."

"Where was Rod during the eighth inning last night?" Nancy asked, closing the magazine.

"Probably icing his arm," Luke said with a shrug. "That's usually what a pitcher does when he's finished on the mound."

"In the locker room?" Nancy asked, her mind working. "Alone?"

"You're thinking Rod could have been in the Freddy the Falcon uniform?" Bess asked.

"It's possible," Nancy said intently. "And if he's jealous of Sean, that gives him a motive for wanting Sean to pitch poorly."

"So we have another suspect," George said. "And someone else for Luke to watch."

"Would you?" Nancy asked.

"Anything to help get Sean's little girl back," Luke said. "But right now I need to go to Sean's. I told him I'd go over this morning."

"We'll meet you at his place," Nancy said. "Delgado said there'd be an agent there, so we can tell him what we've learned."

"But if the kidnappers are watching, won't they get suspicious?" Bess asked, biting her bottom lip.

"Actually, it's best to make it look as if everything is normal. No one knows *we* know what's going on. We're Sean's friends—that's all."

The broken vase was gone and the family room had been straightened up when Nancy and her friends walked into Sean's house. The curtains on the large picture window were closed, blocking the view to the backyard, and a stranger stood in the hallway eyeing Nancy and her friends. He was dressed in shorts and a Falcon T-shirt and held a radio in his hand.

"Meet Russ Nunn," Sean said, gesturing toward the man. "We hope no one else knows he's here—and if anybody does see him, he's an old friend of mine from school."

Nancy knew immediately that Nunn was the FBI agent.

"Hello, Ms. Drew," he said without waiting for an introduction, and then with a nod he acknowledged George, Bess, and Luke by name. Nancy knew Delgado had given him their descriptions. She looked over at the counter where a tape recorder sat beside the telephone.

"Have there been any calls?" she asked Sean.

His expression became even sadder. "No. I can't bear to think where Caitlin was last night."

Nancy was about to say something reassuring, but before she could speak, the doorbell rang.

Russ stared at Sean. "Are you expecting anyone else?" he asked.

"No," Sean replied, walking to the front door as Nunn disappeared down the hallway. The rest of the group waited in the family room. When Sean returned, he was carrying a small, flat box.

"I found it on the doorstep," he said.

Russ poked his head out from the hallway. Immediately his eyes fixed on the box as Sean set it on the coffee table and reached for the lid.

Nancy was beside him in a flash, touching his wrist in a gesture that told him to stop.

"This could be from the kidnappers," she said. "If it is, we need to be very careful we don't destroy any evidence."

"Ms. Drew is right," Russ said, stepping to the other side of Sean. "But first we need to find out who left it." Russ made a quick call on his hand-held radio. "The box was left by a delivery van from River Heights Courier Service," he said. "An agent will check out the driver."

Russ examined the box and began to look around the room. Nancy guessed he was searching for something to use to open the box without touching it. She handed him a pen. With a quick nod of thanks, Russ pushed up the lid.

Inside the box was a lock of fine, dark hair.

Under it was a note in cut-out block letters. As the rest of the group stared, Luke read the words out loud:

Throw the series, or your daughter will lose more than her hair.

Chapter

Eight

SEAN'S FACE turned white. He reached for the lock of hair, and this time it was Russ Nunn's hand that shot out and caught his wrist.

"I'm sorry, but you can't touch it," Russ said. "We'll have to send it to the lab."

Sean slowly let his hand drop to his side as Russ released his grip.

Russ flipped the lid of the box shut, then got back on his radio, reporting to Delgado.

"Isn't it dangerous, using the radio like that?" Bess asked when Russ had finished. "Someone could overhear."

"They're probably using a special scrambled frequency," Nancy suggested as Russ clipped the radio back on his belt.

"That's right," Russ said to Nancy. "Sounds like you know quite a bit about FBI procedure."

"A little," Nancy said, perching herself on one of the stools by the kitchen counter. "And I have a bit more information. I had a visitor this morning." She handed Madeline de Grasse's business card to Russ, glancing at Sean as she did so.

The pitcher was standing between George and Luke, obviously very troubled.

"What's this?" Russ asked, frowning as he took the card from Nancy.

"A Ms. de Grasse came to my house this morning," Nancy explained. "She said she's representing Mr. and Mrs. Zabowski. They're going to try to get custody of Caitlin."

Sean's response was quick and loud. "What do they think they're doing? I'll have their heads for this!"

"Take it easy," Nancy said gently.

"Nancy's right," Luke said, putting his hand on Sean's shoulder. "You have to stay cool. The Zabowskis are just like hecklers—you can't let them get to you."

The baseball comparison worked. Sean sighed and leaned against the counter. "Okay, okay," he said at last. "But I'm going to see them. They're not going to turn Caitlin's disappearance into a three-ring circus—not if I can help it."

"Luke and I'll go with you," Nancy said quickly. "What they say could be important to the case."

"All right," Sean said at last, checking his

watch. "They said they were staying at the River's Edge Lodge. I doubt they'd have gone back to Chicago yet."

"They're at the River's Edge?" Bess said in surprise. "That's where the Rangers are staying. I overheard some fans talking about it at the concession stand."

"Maybe there is a connection between the Zabowskis and baseball," George offered.

"If there is, I'm going to find out what it is," Sean said, his face red with anger.

"Just talk to the Zabowskis," Russ told him. "Anything beyond that, we'll handle."

Sean turned away without answering and strode through the kitchen toward the front door.

Nancy tossed the keys to her Mustang to George and said she'd hook up with them later at the Roost. Then she and Luke followed Sean to his car.

The River's Edge Lodge was the largest hotel and convention center in River Heights. Sean directed Luke to park in the lot and quickly led the way to the main entry. The Zabowskis had given him their room number the night before, so they walked past the registration desk to the elevators. Sean pushed the button for the fourth floor. When they stepped out of the elevator, Nancy was facing a wall of glass that overlooked a well-kept plaza in the triangle formed by the three towers of the hotel complex.

She took a quick peek and then followed Sean and Luke toward the corner room at the end of the hall. Mr. Zabowski answered the door on the second knock.

"You're not welcome here," he growled at Sean, raising his chin slightly as he spoke.

"I don't care if I'm welcome or not," Sean said. Pushing Mr. Zabowski aside, he strode into the room. Nancy and Luke followed.

"I know you hired a lawyer," Sean announced.

"We're just doing what's best for our granddaughter," Mr. Zabowski said. "You obviously can't take care of her while you're running around the country playing baseball."

"But, Mr. Zabowski," Nancy pleaded as she squeezed past Sean into the spacious room. "Don't you realize that once you go to court, the press will get hold of this and Caitlin could be in even more danger?"

"Don't be ridiculous," Mrs. Zabowski interrupted. "We told our attorney to be absolutely discreet. Nothing will be done to put Caitlin at risk."

"She told Nancy that she was going to file the petition as soon as she could," Sean said, taking a step closer to Bert. Caitlin's grandfather moved back and bumped into the couch.

Nancy saw the Zabowskis exchange glances and thought there was a trace of uneasiness in both their faces.

"Don't try to blame this on us," Mrs. Zabowski said loudly. "It's not our fault that Caitlin's in danger. It's you and your miserable job that caused this." Her face had become bright

71

pink, and she shook her finger at Sean. "Traveling around and having your name and picture in the paper so much, you made yourself a target. You made *Caitlin* a target."

"But, Mrs. Zabowski," Nancy began, "couldn't all this wait until Caitlin is safely back home?"

Nancy wanted to defuse the tension in the room before things got out of hand. She turned to Luke for help, but he, too, was flushed with anger.

"You make it sound like we're criminals," Luke said. He stepped up beside Sean. "Baseball's the all-American sport. You ought to be proud."

"Please," Nancy said, stepping between the Zabowskis and Sean and Luke. "If any of you truly care about Caitlin you'll realize this is not the time for a fight."

"She's right," Bert finally admitted. "All this will keep until Caitlin is back. I'll call off the lawyer and make sure she keeps quiet. She shouldn't have acted so hastily anyway."

Mrs. Zabowski moved closer to her husband and slipped her hand into the crook of his elbow.

Sean sighed. "Let's go," he said at last. "Before I take a swing at someone."

Nancy was following the two baseball players through the door when Mrs. Zabowski spoke again. Her voice was softer, though still not friendly. "Sean, we really are trying to do what's best for Caitlin."

Sean turned around. "Caitlin is my daughter," he rasped. "Taking her away from me is the worst thing you could do." With that, he headed out the door.

"It's almost as if they haven't accepted the fact that Caitlin's been kidnapped," Luke said as they waited for the elevator. "Their only concern is getting custody."

"Yes," Nancy agreed, letting her gaze drift to the large windows and the plaza below. She turned back when the elevator arrived. "But it's possible they're just very upset. Sean, did you know they wanted Caitlin to live with them?"

Sean nodded and let out a sigh as the elevator doors whispered closed behind them. "Last winter they offered to keep Caitlin during baseball season. They know it's hard for me to take care of her when I travel." Sean shrugged and watched the numbers flash above the elevator doors. "Stella even suggested that Caitlin could stay with them all the time."

"You said no," Nancy prompted.

"Yes, and not very nicely," Sean said, folding his arms at his chest. "I was pretty angry. Caitlin and I have a special relationship. She lost her mother. It would be terrible for her if she lost me, too."

"After that, did they ever say anything more about keeping her?" Nancy asked.

"No," Sean replied, shaking his head. "Not until now."

"They *did* promise to call off the lawyer," she offered.

"True," Luke said as the elevator reached the main floor and the doors slid open. "Look, Sean, why don't I spend the afternoon with you at your place. That Nunn guy doesn't look like great company."

"You don't have to," Sean replied.

"I know I don't. But I want to," Luke stated flatly.

"I'd like to make one more stop while we're here," Nancy said. She led the way to the main desk where a lone clerk stood behind the counter. "I want to send some flowers to Stormy Tarver," Nancy said politely to the clerk. "She is staying here, isn't she?"

The young woman punched some keys on her computer. "Yes," she said.

Luke and Sean acted surprised as they waited a few yards from the counter.

"Good, can you tell me her room number?" Nancy said.

"I'm afraid I can't give out that information. Just have the flowers delivered here, and I'll send them up," the clerk said.

"Thank you," Nancy said. There was still no one else around to help the clerk, so Nancy decided to make her move. Turning her back to the clerk, she mouthed the words *Get her out of the way* to Sean and Luke. It took Luke only a moment to react.

"Excuse me," he said brightly, stepping up to

the counter. "I want to buy a present for my girlfriend. Is there a gift shop in the hotel?"

"Of course," the clerk said helpfully. "It's just down the—"

Luke cut her off immediately. "I'm just no good with directions," he said with a charming smile. "Could you show me the way?"

"Certainly," the young woman said, moving out from behind her counter. Luke leaned close to her and smiled warmly.

That was the moment Nancy had been waiting for. She jumped and caught herself on the edge of the massive hotel counter. Leaning over as far as she could, she was able to get a glimpse of the computer screen the clerk had been working at. She was in luck. The woman hadn't cleared the screen after looking up Stormy Tarver. Nancy could see the room assignment—814. She hopped back down to the floor just as Luke thanked the clerk and turned around. She let Luke and Sean walk halfway across the lobby toward the gift shop before catching up to them.

"You're pretty quick," Nancy whispered to Luke as she stepped beside him.

"Thanks," said Luke with a wry smile.

"I doubt you're sending flowers to Stormy," Sean said, "so you must consider her a suspect. Did you get her room number?"

"Yes. She's in 814," Nancy said as they continued down the hall to the gift shop.

"Is that important?" Luke asked.

"It could be," Nancy said. "It's the same

number that was on a piece of paper Rod Sanders dropped at the ballpark last night."

"Rod Sanders had Stormy Tarver's room number?" Sean said, surprised.

"Quite a coincidence, right?" Nancy commented.

"But why would Rod be talking to the owner of the Rangers during the series?" Luke asked.

"Why, indeed," said Nancy.

When they reached the gift shop, they paused. Farther down the hall Nancy noticed a side exit that looked as if it led to the parking lot. Nancy headed for it and was about to push through the door when she stopped dead in her tracks. There, in a newspaper box, was that day's paper. As Nancy read the headline, she could hardly believe her eyes.

It said, Do or Die Championship—Desperate Stormy May Lose Team.

Chapter

Nine

Could Stormy be desperate enough to kidnap Caitlin?

Nancy dug in her purse for some change, but Luke was ahead of her. After drawing some change out of his pocket, he deposited it in the box and opened the lid.

Nancy grabbed a paper and pushed through the door. Sean was close behind her, reading over her shoulder as they made their way to Luke's car. Once inside, Nancy read aloud from the article.

In addition to the same rumors about Stormy's finances Bess had overheard at the ballpark the night before, the paper also reported that the Rangers owner was in the middle of negotiating for a television contract for the next season. That contract could be worth hundreds of thousands of dollars, the article said, enough to get Stormy out of her financial hole and save the team. But the television station was only interested if the Rangers won the series.

"That sure gives her a motive," Luke commented when Nancy finished reading.

"It could," she said.

The three of them stopped at a drive-in several blocks down from the River's Edge. Over burgers and fries, Luke continued to talk about Stormy. Sean was quiet. When they were finished with lunch, Luke dropped off Nancy at her house. She told the guys that she'd see them at the game later, waved goodbye, and jogged up the walk.

Inside, she headed straight for the phone and dialed George's number. Bess was with her cousin. Nancy told them everything that had happened at the hotel, then asked them to pick her up right away. "I've got a suspect to check out," she explained.

"No problem," George replied.

Ten minutes later Nancy heard a horn and dashed out the front door. When she reached her car, George scooted over so that she could drive.

"Where to now?" Bess asked.

"I want to check out Rebecca's apartment," Nancy said, taking her notebook out of her purse. "Let's see if we can find it."

It took Nancy only a few minutes to drive to the run-down apartment complex where Rebecca lived. She wondered if Delgado had already posted an agent there. If so, would he let them in? Of course, the FBI was supposed to be keeping a low profile, so maybe they'd let her do as she wished.

"Watch for building G," Nancy said as she turned into the long driveway. The apartment buildings showed all the signs of age and neglect —peeling paint, missing shingles, and overgrown flower beds.

"There it is," Bess said, pointing to a large wooden *G* hanging on one of the buildings. Nancy quickly parked the car, crossed the lawn, and climbed to the second floor. On the landing at the top of the stairs, Nancy found her first clue.

"Gray clay," George said as Nancy pointed it out. "Is that important?"

"I don't know," Nancy said. "But there was gray clay by the side door of Sean's garage yesterday."

Nancy knocked on the apartment door and waited several minutes before pulling out her lock-pick kit from her pocket. "Tell me if anyone comes," she said quietly before going to work.

In a moment the door swung open and Nancy peeked in at an empty studio apartment with a tiny kitchenette at one end.

"It won't take long to check out this place," Bess joked as she and George followed Nancy into the room.

Nancy glanced behind her one last time before closing the door. No one had seen them go in. She stood still just inside the door, her sharp eyes taking in every detail of the apartment.

"That must be Rebecca," she said, pointing to

a picture on the coffee table. It was a shot of a young woman with short red hair and a bright smile.

"It fits the description Luke gave us," George confirmed.

"That's not all," Bess stammered, her eyes getting big. She stepped over to the picture to look more closely. "She's wearing a Falcons' concession stand uniform."

"Are you sure?" George asked, joining her friends by the picture. "All you can see is the shirt collar."

"You can see part of the Falcon emblem," Nancy said, pointing to the tiny embroidered image of Freddy the Falcon.

"Why didn't Sean tell us she worked at the stadium?" George asked.

"Maybe he didn't know," Nancy said, straightening up. "It could be an old picture."

"Maybe she was fired and has a grudge against the Falcons," Bess suggested excitedly.

"That's speculation," Nancy said. "But we'll have to check it out."

"I can help with that," Bess said. "I'll ask around at work tonight."

"Good idea," Nancy said. "Now let's see what else we can find." She pulled a handkerchief from her pocket and wrapped it around the knob on the drawer of the end table. Inside, Nancy found a stack of papers.

"They look like bills," George said as Nancy

turned over each paper, using the handkerchief to avoid leaving prints.

"Past-due bills," Bess added. "I guess Rebecca has money problems."

She continued leafing through the stack, then stopped when she came to a half-written letter.

"I've seen this handwriting before," she said, pulling out the letter and laying it on top of the table. "I bet it matches the shopping list we found at Sean's. The FBI will be able to say for sure."

Nancy folded up the letter and put it into her pocket. She checked the tiny bathroom next and poked through each cupboard in the kitchen, but found nothing else interesting.

"Well, we found two clues anyway," Bess said as Nancy carefully closed the door. "The letter and the unpaid bills."

"Three, counting the clay," George added.

"Yes," Nancy said as they descended the stairs. "But remember, sometimes what you don't find can be just as important as what you do."

Bess and George wanted to know what else she had discovered. Nancy was about to explain when she nearly bumped into a plump, silver-haired woman in thick glasses who was on her way up the steps.

"You must have come to see Rebecca Carter," the woman said, eyeing the girls suspiciously.

"What makes you say that?" Nancy asked.

"Because you're coming down the stairs, and

only Rebecca and I live up there," the woman said. "You didn't come to see me, did you?"

"Rebecca was supposed to meet us for lunch today, and she didn't show," Nancy said. "Do you know where she might be?"

"No, but you're the second set of visitors Rebecca has had today," she said. "Unusual for such a loner."

"Really?" Nancy said. "Who else was here?"

"Two young ladies," the woman said. She cocked her head to one side as though suddenly realizing something of great importance. "They were in her apartment this morning. But it's funny, I didn't see Rebecca. In fact, I saw her leave yesterday, and I didn't see her come back."

"What did her other visitors look like?" Nancy asked. "Maybe I know them."

"Well, I'm pretty sure one of them had brown hair," the woman said, her eyes narrowing to slits. "But it could have been blond. And the other one was wearing shorts and a shirt—white, I think, or maybe blue."

Bess turned her head just enough so the woman couldn't see her when she rolled her eyes.

Nancy thanked the woman warmly and went to her car.

"Who do you suppose was in Rebecca's apartment this morning," Bess whispered as they climbed into the Mustang.

"The FBI, maybe," Nancy said, wondering what the agents might have found.

"I'm supposed to be at the ballpark in forty-five minutes," Bess said. "Could we swing by my place so I can get into my uniform?"

Nancy agreed. While she and George waited for Bess, they talked about the case. They planned to eat dinner at the stadium during the game. It took Bess almost half an hour to change. Back in the car on the way to the Roost, Bess started to get nervous about being late. "I knew I should have ironed this blouse earlier," she fretted. "But maybe I'll still be on time."

She was checking her watch for the third time when Nancy pulled up to an intersection. A large truck hauling lumber was making a slow turn, blocking their way.

"Now we missed the light," Bess said as the signal turned red. "And this is not a good day to make my supervisor unhappy. I wanted to ask her about Rebecca."

"I think this is a bad-luck intersection," George said. "This is the same place the concrete truck nearly hit us yesterday."

"Yes," Nancy said as the light turned green again. "There must be some construction going on west of town."

A few minutes later Nancy pulled her car into the Roost parking lot. Bess hurried toward her concession stand, and George followed Nancy to the locker rooms.

"I want to see if I can talk to Rod Sanders before the game," Nancy said, taking long strides. "He's the one who recommended Rebecca to Sean."

"How are you going to talk to Rod without telling him about the kidnapping?" George asked.

"I thought I could pretend to be a free-lance writer," Nancy said. "With Luke's help it just might work."

Nancy and George found a batboy to take a message into the locker room to Luke, but they had to wait almost fifteen minutes before he came out.

"We were having a team meeting," he explained, flashing a smile in George's direction. "Barrows is trying to get everyone psyched up for this one."

He agreed to tell Rod that Nancy was a free-lance journalist.

Nancy and George waited while Luke went back into the locker room. When he reappeared, Rod wasn't with him.

"I don't understand it," Luke said. "He refused to come out, and he never turns down interviews."

"Maybe he didn't believe I was a reporter," Nancy said quietly.

"No, that wasn't it," Luke said. "He just doesn't want to talk to reporters. He said you could call him next week."

"It almost sounds like he has something to hide," George remarked.

Nancy was about to agree when the locker room door swung open with such force that it slammed into the wall with a crash. An angry

Sean Reeves strode through the door and grabbed Nancy by the shoulder. He steered her forcefully down the corridor to a quiet corner and pushed her up against the wall.

"Listen and listen good!" he said. "I want you off this case, and the FBI, too. I want you all to get out of my life!"

Chapter

Ten

STARING INTO Sean's anguished eyes, Nancy knew immediately that something awful had happened.

"Okay," she said carefully. "If you're sure that's what you want, I'll back off. But first let's talk."

Sean took his hands off her shoulders and tipped his head back in a way that told Nancy he was trying to get himself under control.

"Tell me what happened," she coaxed gently.

"I got another phone call," he said, still gazing toward the ceiling. "It was Caitlin." He lowered his head and put both hands up to his face. "She was crying."

Nancy waited, afraid to speak or even to move for fear Sean would stop talking.

"She kept saying she wanted to come home," he said, his voice cracking. "She begged me not to tell anyone. She said if I tell, she can't come home."

Nancy's mind was racing. She knew the call had terrified Sean, but it gave her new hope. At least Caitlin was all right.

"When did you get the call?" she asked.

"Just now," he replied, finally looking at Nancy. "In Barrows's office."

"Did Barrows take the call?" Nancy pressed. Sean nodded.

"Did he talk to Caitlin?"

"No," Sean said. "He said it was some guy, then when I got there, Caitlin was on the line."

Nancy quickly considered her male suspects. It couldn't have been Rod Sanders or Bill Barrows. Both of them had been in the locker room. So who could have made the call?

"Listen carefully," Nancy said firmly. "Some guy has Caitlin and he doesn't know you've told anyone or you wouldn't have gotten that call. Are you sure you want me off the case?"

Sean gazed up at the ceiling again, then shook his head. "No," he said. "I'm not sure of anything, except that I want my little girl back."

"Then you've got to give us more time."

Sean took a deep breath, pressing his eyes closed for a moment. "Okay," he whispered at last.

Nancy turned away from him long enough to observe Luke and George watching from down the corridor. Nancy nodded to them, and Luke came over quickly to stand beside Sean. Nancy took a deep breath. "You two have a ballgame to play," she said, trying to sound as upbeat as she could.

"She's right," Luke said, slapping Sean lightly on the shoulder.

"Yeah, I know," Sean said tonelessly. The two players were almost to the locker room door when Sean turned around. "Thanks, Nancy," he said, and then he was gone.

"What was that all about?" George asked.

"Sean got another phone call," Nancy said. "He's scared."

George shook her head sadly. "Is he going to throw another game?"

"I think so," Nancy said. "The note yesterday said he had to lose the whole series."

"Well, Nancy Drew, fancy meeting you here."

Nancy saw Brenda Carlton strolling down the corridor.

"Are you really only here to watch the ballgame?" Brenda asked, eyeing Nancy suspiciously.

"Sure," Nancy said brightly. "What else is there?"

"A mystery maybe," Brenda said. "Involving a certain baseball player?"

Nancy felt a lump form in her throat, but she kept smiling. "You must know something I don't," she said. "What's going on?"

Brenda stuck the reporter's notebook she'd been holding into a pocket of her shoulder bag. "I heard from an anonymous source that the FBI is in town and that they're investigating the play-offs."

"Really? How exciting," Nancy said, trying not to show her shock. "What type of case is it?"

"That's the mystery," Brenda said, flipping her hair over her shoulder. "Well, I guess you really don't know anything, then. Too bad. It sounds like a big case."

"I'm sure you'll solve it," Nancy replied, though Brenda didn't seem to notice the trace of sarcasm that had crept into her voice.

"I'm sure I will, too," Brenda said, leaving. "Just keep watching the paper."

Nancy swallowed hard. She started down the corridor toward the stairway that led to the inside of the stadium.

"That sounds like trouble," George commented.

"It sure does," Nancy agreed, stepping into the stream of fans heading for the bleachers. "And knowing Brenda, she won't think twice about putting this in the paper if she figures it out."

Once again Luke had gotten them front row seats in the section above the stadium boxes.

Nancy felt a deep sadness as she watched the players warming up on the field below. Sean had come to River Heights to try to get his game back together and save his career. Instead, he was being forced to throw lousy pitches to save his daughter's life.

"I wish I could get excited," George said solemnly. "I can't believe the series is tied and we're sitting here with no hope the Falcons will actually win the championship."

"I know what you mean," Nancy said. "Let's see if we can spot Stormy Tarver," she said, turning her mind back to the case. She located Stormy near her box, gleefully working the crowd. Twice Nancy saw her put her arms around a fan to pose for a photograph.

"She looks awfully confident," George said.

"No kidding," Nancy replied.

When the game started, the Falcons took an early lead with two runs in the second inning, but they had to struggle as the Rangers scored three in the fifth.

Nancy watched the gum-chewing Bill Barrows urge his team on, but without much enthusiasm, it seemed. She remembered Luke's description of him as a sad old veteran possibly facing the end of his career. She hoped he wouldn't be too hard on Sean.

The Falcons managed to hold the score at two to three until the seventh inning when Sean grimly took the mound. He walked the first batter and watched the second Ranger hit his fastball into center field for a double. One strike-out and a sacrifice fly left the Rangers with two outs and runners on second and third. When the next batter hit a line drive to score two runs, Barrows came to life. He jumped off the bench and threw his cap on the ground before calling time out and stomping out to the pitcher's mound. After much arm waving, Barrows retreated to the sidelines and Sean threw three strikes.

Then it was the Falcons' turn to bat. They quickly got two runners on base with only one out.

"Oh, Nancy, what do you think he's going to do," George said, putting her hand on Nancy's arm.

Nancy looked up from her bag of peanuts to see Luke walking to the plate.

"I don't know," Nancy whispered. "But I'm glad I'm not in his place."

Nancy knew Luke was committed to baseball and to his team. But she also knew he cared enough about Sean and Caitlin to understand that the Falcons had to lose. She wondered if he would really try his hardest at bat.

"Strike two!" the empire yelled as the ball whizzed past a second time. Luke walked a slow circle before coming back to the plate and sending the third pitch on a wobbly ride to first base, where he was tagged out.

The team struggled on until a Falcon rally in the bottom of the eighth inning gave the River Heights team the lead by two runs. The crowd yelled and whistled its approval.

When Sean took the mound in the ninth, Nancy knew that all he had to do to assure a Falcon win was keep the Rangers from scoring. Sean quickly allowed four hits and a Ranger run.

The Falcon fans saw their victory slipping away and started yelling for a new pitcher.

Nancy noticed Sean glance toward the stands. Then Luke called time out and walked to the mound.

"I wonder what he's saying," George said tensely.

Luke returned to his spot behind the plate and Sean struck out the batter with a perfect knuckleball. As he prepared to make his next pitch, the Ranger runner on first took off to steal second base.

Sean reacted quickly, but instead of his usual perfect throw, the ball went way out of reach of the second baseman. The runner slid into second base safely.

"Get that bozo off the field!" Nancy heard someone scream from near her in the stands. Immediately a wave of boos went up from the crowd. Coffee cups, wadded-up popcorn bags, and apple cores all began to fly onto the field.

Sean waited for the ball to come back from center field and then dropped his head as he turned around to face the next batter. After that, Sean pitched the worst game of his career, allowing hit after hit until the Rangers were ahead by two runs.

The Falcons didn't score their last time at bat, and the Rangers' bagged another victory.

"Tomorrow's a day off, but if the Rangers win on Wednesday, they'll take the series," George said as she and Nancy stood up to leave.

More than anything in the world, Nancy

wanted to find Caitlin and solve this mystery in time for Sean to have a chance to play his best.

"Maybe Bess has some news about Rebecca," George said hopefully. They fought the milling crowd down the corridor to the concession stand where Bess was working.

"It's going to be a while," Bess said when they arrived. "I've got clean-up duty."

Nancy and George each took a snow cone back into the stands and watched the stadium crew sweep the garbage off the field. When they returned to the concession stand almost thirty minutes later, Bess was just finishing up. She slipped out and said excitedly, "You won't believe what I've learned. Rebecca is a thief!"

Chapter

Eleven

"HOW DO YOU KNOW?" George asked.

Half whispering as they walked down the empty corridors toward the exit, Bess replied, "I managed to get my supervisor, Carolyn Flynne, talking during one of our slow times. She said she remembered Rebecca from when she worked here last season."

"What else?" Nancy asked. "Why did she quit?"

"She didn't quit," Bess said, her eyes round. "Well, technically she did, but only after Carolyn caught her stealing from the cash register and threatened to call the police."

George let out a low whistle.

"Carolyn also said that Rebecca was rude and tried to shortchange customers," Bess went on.

"Are you sure it's the same Rebecca?" George

asked in disbelief. "Sean said his Rebecca was friendly and good with Caitlin."

"No, it was definitely Rebecca Carter," Bess insisted. "I even had Carolyn describe her. Besides, remember the photo of her in the uniform?"

Nancy suddenly stopped walking. "Rod Sanders recommended Rebecca to Sean. I wonder if he knew about her past."

"Carolyn said only management knew," Bess answered. "And she made me promise not to spread it around since Rebecca was never charged with a crime."

"Could Carolyn have been wrong about her stealing?" Nancy asked.

"She said she actually saw her take a handful of bills out of the register and stuff them into her pocket," Bess said. "It happened right after the stand closed, and Carolyn hadn't counted the money yet."

"Do you think Rod recommended Rebecca to Sean so she could help with the kidnapping?" George asked, turning to Nancy.

"Possibly," Nancy said, continuing on toward the door that led to the locker room exit, which was close to where she'd parked her car. "Or maybe Rod set Rebecca up knowing she lived alone and no one would miss her if she disappeared along with Caitlin."

"So Rebecca could be a victim," Bess said.

"Yes," Nancy answered. "But whether she is or isn't, she's an important key to this puzzle."

The door to the Falcon locker room had been propped open, and Nancy could see that the interior was dark. She was just moving past it when she heard a series of heavy metallic clicks that sounded like a locker door opening. She stopped and listened.

"What is it?" Bess asked.

"I'm not sure," Nancy whispered back, then raised a finger to her lips as she took a single step inside the dark locker room. At the far end she saw the bobbing beam of a flashlight. Then, very faintly, she heard more of the metallic clicks and scratches. Nancy straightened and tensed. Someone was definitely in there.

Nancy motioned for Bess and George to wait outside, then cautiously moved into the darkness, feeling her way past lockers and benches, inching her way toward the bobbing light. With searching fingers, she found the cold metal of a bank of lockers and slid silently behind them until she was just around the corner from the beam of the flashlight.

Her eyes had become accustomed to the darkness, and as she peered around the corner, she saw a dark figure not more than ten feet from her. The person was putting something in one of the lockers. It was Stormy Tarver.

Nancy stood stone still as Stormy eased the locker shut with barely a sound, slipped the padlock back in place, and latched it. Then Stormy started for the exit.

Nancy waited. After a long moment she stole

toward the spot where Stormy had been, slipped off the light jacket she had been wearing, and dropped it silently to the floor to mark the locker that Stormy had opened.

Suddenly Nancy heard Bess shriek. She dashed toward the sound, but stopped well inside the door.

"What are you doing here?" Stormy snapped.

"We could ask you the same thing," George returned.

Nancy flattened herself against the wall just around the corner from her friends and listened. She didn't want Stormy to know she had been in the locker room.

"It's none of your business," Stormy snapped.

When Nancy peeked around the corner of the doorway a moment later, Stormy was walking away while George and Bess watched.

"What happened?" Nancy asked.

"She ran right into me," Bess said angrily.

"Bess was listening in the doorway," George whispered with a hint of a smile.

"Good work." Nancy laughed. "I would love to have seen Stormy's face."

"But what was she doing in the locker room?" George asked.

"She put something in one of the lockers," Nancy said. "The player must have given her his combination, because there was a padlock on it. Or maybe she's good at picking locks."

"Whose locker?" Bess asked anxiously.

"I don't know," Nancy said. "But I can find

out." She led the way back into the darkness. Finding a switch by the door, she flipped on the light. Now she could see the two long rows of lockers and the wooden benches in between.

She walked down the row to where her jacket lay on the floor and looked up at locker number 39. It was locked with a combination padlock, and just above the lock was a big dent. Nancy touched the dent with her finger.

"Rod bashed his locker when he found out Sean was coming to play with the Falcons," George said.

"I remember," Nancy replied, then examined the padlock, spinning the dial lightly in her fingers. She narrowed her eyes and carefully began to turn the dial first to the right, then to the left, then to the right again. Each time she waited until she could feel the tumblers drop into place. After the third turn, Nancy stopped. She took a deep breath as she looked from George to Bess. George gave her a thumbs-up sign, and Nancy pulled on the padlock.

"It worked," Bess said as the metal loop slipped from the lock.

Nancy breathed a sigh of relief. "Okay," she said. "Let's see what's inside."

The contents of the locker were neatly organized. A pair of baseball shoes was in the bottom, a Falcons jersey and hat hung on a hook on one side of the locker, and a baseball mitt was on the other. Nancy had to stretch to look on the shelf above the hooks. There she saw a sheet of white paper. She pulled it out, holding only one edge, and saw that it was a piece of stationery from the River's Edge Lodge. Written on it in flowing script were the words, We need to meet. Name the time, same place.

"Stormy Tarver is meeting with a Falcon player?" Bess asked. "But who and why?"

"I can answer the first part of that," George said. She reached into the locker and grabbed one sleeve of the baseball jersey, stretching it out so the number and name on the back were clearly visible. The number was 46 and the name above it, in bright blue letters, was Sanders.

"Stormy Tarver is meeting with Rod Sanders," Nancy said as George released the jersey. "I only wish we knew when and where."

"We could tail one of them," Bess offered.

"That could tie us up for days," Nancy said. "Besides, if they spotted us, it might put Caitlin into more danger."

"So what are we going to do?" George asked, leaning against the lockers.

"We'll let someone else follow them," Nancy said. "Someone with lots of manpower."

"The FBI," Bess said, sitting down on the bench.

Nancy nodded. She put the paper back on the shelf and closed the locker, replacing the padlock just as Stormy Tarver had done.

"I'll call Chief McGinnis," Nancy said. "He'll get the word to Delgado, and the FBI can take it from there." Nancy picked up her jacket and glanced around the locker room to make sure nothing was out of place. Then she followed Bess and George out the door and flicked off the light.

Nancy was awake early the next morning. Even though there wouldn't be another baseball game until the following evening, she had plenty to do. She'd spoken with Chief McGinnis the night before, but she still needed to call Stormy Tarver and then meet with George, Bess, Luke, and Sean.

She was heading for the den to make her call when Carson Drew stopped her on his way to work. He was carrying his briefcase in one hand and a bag of clothes in the other.

"Going to the big game tomorrow?" he asked.

Nancy grimaced, then nodded. She didn't have time to tell him what a disaster the championship series had become.

"Would you mind dropping these off at Haven House for me?" he said, handing her the bag. "They're collecting clothes for the homeless this week."

"Sure," Nancy said. She walked her father to his car, kissed him goodbye, and put the bag of clothes on the backseat of her Mustang before hurrying back inside. In the quiet of the den she dialed the number for the River's Edge Lodge and asked for room 814.

The phone rang five times before Stormy answered with a gruff hello.

"Ms. Tarver, I'm Nancy Drew, a free-lance writer," Nancy began brightly.

"Good morning," Stormy said, her voice suddenly friendly. "What can I do for you?"

"I'm doing a series of articles on powerful women in sports," Nancy said. "Of course, it wouldn't be complete without an interview with you."

"Who are you writing for?" Stormy asked.

Nancy paused. *"American Sports* wants it," she fibbed, "but I may just shop it around."

"Fine," Stormy said. "I always have time for the press, but it'll have to be this evening, say around five, here at the lodge? Why don't you meet me in the restaurant?"

"Great," Nancy said. As she hung up, she thanked her lucky stars that Stormy Tarver was such a publicity hound, and that she had not shown her face to Stormy in the locker room the night before.

Nancy left the den, had breakfast and a shower, said goodbye to Hannah, and headed for her car. She had just enough time to meet her friends at Andy's Arcade for the early lunch they had arranged the day before. Nancy had a lot of information she wanted to go over with her friends, and she was hoping that the atmosphere at Andy's would cheer up Sean.

The arcade was a dozen blocks from the Roost, next to a grocery store that was already teeming with customers. Nancy had to park her Mustang three shops down from Andy's. She had just locked her car and stepped onto the sidewalk when she sensed someone right behind her. Instinctively she tried to move away, but felt a strong hand on her shoulder.

"Don't turn around," a man's voice ordered in a commanding whisper. "And keep walking."

Chapter

Twelve

"You don't know who I am, do you?" the stranger asked as they continued down the sidewalk. There was a hint of satisfaction in his voice.

"No," she answered, feeling adrenaline flow through her.

"Delgado," he whispered. "We need to talk."

Nancy's fear drained away. She tried to turn around again, but again Delgado stopped her.

"After I leave, get back into your car and drive north on Tatum Avenue for two blocks, take a left, and turn into the first parking lot you come to. There will be a mover's van there. Park and get out."

The pressure on Nancy's shoulder vanished. She took two more steps and turned around in time to see Delgado, dressed in a light shirt and pants, slip into a blue car that pulled away from the curb. Then, throwing a quick glance toward Andy's Arcade, she went back to her car. Her friends would have to wait.

Nancy's excitement grew as she drove down Tatum Avenue. She couldn't wait for the chance to compare notes with the FBI. Only one thing bothered her—she had the uncomfortable feeling that Delgado had enjoyed toying with her at the mall.

The lot Delgado had directed her to was a little-used gravel area with a fringe of weeds along one edge. Nancy pulled her Mustang up beside the moving van and was climbing out when she heard Delgado's voice for the second time.

She turned to see him standing at the back of the truck, motioning for her to follow him. He disappeared around the corner. Nancy followed. He was holding open a door in the rear of the van. She stepped inside, expecting a dark and shabby interior. Instead, she found herself in an ultramodern FBI mobile command center.

Victor motioned Nancy to a folding chair by a narrow table set up in the center of the van. Except for the spot where Nancy sat, the table was covered with papers, laid out in an orderly fashion. On the wall was a large bulletin board with the days of the week listed across the top and notes tacked under each day. Behind Nancy was a map cluttered with colored pins. Toward the front of the truck another agent with a radio headset was talking into a microphone and taking notes. This, Nancy guessed, was the dispatcher Russ Nunn had been talking to when he radioed from Sean's house.

Delgado pulled up a chair across the table from Nancy. "The note you found in the locker room definitely sounds interesting," he said seriously. "Was there anything more than the meeting request?"

"No," Nancy said. "As I told Chief McGinnis on the phone, the words were written in blue ink on a piece of stationery from the River's Edge Lodge."

"We've been watching both Stormy and Rod Sanders ever since you called," Victor said, staring into Nancy's eyes. "So far neither has made a move."

"What about the lock of hair that was delivered to Sean?" Nancy asked. "Did you get any information from that?"

Victor shook his head. "Nothing very useful."

"But something," Nancy persisted.

Victor shrugged and gave Nancy a sideways look that said she wasn't behaving properly. "We did match the hair to a sample from Caitlin's brush, and the handwriting on the note matches the one Sean got from the bird on the mound."

"What about the box?" Nancy tried again. "Were there prints?" She had been hoping she and Delgado could help each other. Now the agent seemed to be holding out on her.

"The only prints were from the delivery boy,"

Victor said, his voice rising impatiently. "He said the box was left outside the office with some money and instructions. No one at the courier service saw who put it there."

Nancy sighed. This was harder than interviewing a suspect.

"What about Rebecca?" she asked, trying to keep her voice friendly. "Have you found her family?"

"Yes, her parents are in New Hampshire," Victor said brusquely. "They didn't know anything, but they're coming here. And now, if you don't mind, I'll ask the questions."

Nancy frowned and leaned back in her chair.

Victor seemed to relax. "I want to know what else you've stumbled across."

"I found out that Rebecca was forced to leave a job at the Roost after she was caught stealing from the cash register at a concession stand," Nancy said stiffly. "It's possible she's not a victim after all."

There was a flash of interest in Victor's eyes. "We learned the same thing," he said, sounding almost friendly. "We also found out that was the second time she had to leave a job for stealing."

"When was the first time?" Nancy asked excitedly, forgetting for a moment that she wasn't supposed to ask questions.

Victor's frown returned. "Six months ago she worked as a clerk in a clothing store," he growled. "The manager caught her taking money from the till. Same as the Roost, basically."

Nancy longed for a few more details, but Victor wasn't offering them. "Then she really is a thief," she said calmly.

"That doesn't mean she's a kidnapper, though," Victor said, lecturing her.

"I know," Nancy said simply. "She could have been set up, but I began to doubt that theory after I saw her apartment."

Victor eyed her suspiciously.

"I know you were there, too," Nancy said. She'd finally had enough of Victor's overbearing manner.

Victor leaned back so that the front legs of his chair came off the floor, and rolled his eyes at the ceiling.

"I went there yesterday," Nancy said coldly. "I picked up a writing sample you can use—if you need it." Her statement seemed to take Victor by surprise. The front legs of his chair hit the floor with a thud.

"We have our own," Victor said wryly. Nancy saw the twinkle in his eye and his tone seemed to soften slightly. "We lifted prints and a handwriting sample from her apartment that confirmed the shopping list you found was written by her. Unfortunately, that doesn't help us much."

"But there was another interesting thing I found in her apartment," Nancy said. "There were no Yummy Bunnies there, so I doubt she bought them for herself."

Victor studied his folded hands, a smile creeping over his lips. "I guess McGinnis was right about you," he said, shaking his head slowly. "And Nunn, too. He said you were a pretty sharp cookie after you figured out his radio system."

"You didn't look for Yummy Bunnies, did you?" Nancy guessed, hoping her observation would not make him angry.

Victor shook his head, and then grabbed a yellow notepad and pencil. "You beat me on the Yummy Bunnies," he said. "So what do we have?"

Nancy felt like shouting for joy. The ice between them had been broken, and Victor was taking her seriously.

"Rebecca could have made the shopping list while getting ready to keep Caitlin," Nancy said. "And what about the clay? There was gray clay at both Sean's house and Rebecca's apartment."

"The two samples matched," Victor said, raising his pencil. "Unfortunately, although clay is unusual in this area, it's not rare enough to match to any one location."

"Is there anything new on the Zabowskis?" Nancy asked, leaning forward.

"We're still following them, but they're moving down on our suspect list," Delgado said. "They haven't done anything suspicious, and we know neither of them left the package with the lock of Caitlin's hair, because we were following them at the time."

"I guess you heard about the call Sean got last night?" Nancy pressed.

Victor scowled. "We put a recorder on the

phone in the locker room early this morning," he said.

Nancy raised her eyebrows but decided not to comment. "All right," she said after a pause, "that leaves Stormy, Rod, and Rebecca as suspects, but unless one of them makes a move, we're no closer to solving this than we were two days ago."

"I agree," Victor said, turning grim.

"I have a meeting with Stormy at five," Nancy said smugly. "I told her I'm a reporter. Maybe I can find out something that will break this case."

"Good luck," Victor said, rising from his chair. "I wish I'd thought of that."

"Thanks," Nancy said, pushing her own chair back. "And one more thing, how did you find me at the mall?"

Victor took the two steps to the door but didn't open it. "Guess," he said, grinning.

"You've been following me," Nancy said, watching his expression. "But for how long?"

"Since you left the parking garage on Sunday night. Don't worry, though, you're not a suspect," Victor said. "I just want to keep you out of trouble."

Nancy swallowed hard. She knew the FBI was doing its job, but still she felt angry. She could feel the blood rush into her face and her cheeks turn bright red. It was as though the spark of friendship between them had just been doused.

"Sorry," Victor said apologetically, seeing her anger rise. "But I didn't know who I was dealing with when I met you. You could have turned out to be a loose cannon."

"Then you agree that I'm not," Nancy snapped.

"Now, wait a minute," Victor said, raising his hands in the air. "I didn't say that. I'm just not so sure anymore."

"So you don't mind if I interview Stormy?"

"Not as long as you tell me what she says," Victor replied.

"I'm sure we can find a way to meet," Nancy said lightly, reaching for the door.

"I don't suppose you'd pay any attention if I told you to be careful?" Victor said smoothly.

"I think anyone would be careful if she knew she had the FBI on her tail," Nancy replied, stepping out of the van. When she turned the corner, she peeked back and saw Victor smiling at her.

Nancy found herself watching her rearview mirror as she drove back to Andy's Arcade. She saw nothing suspicious. Still, the idea that she had been followed for two days without knowing it was hard for her to take.

She pulled into the strip mall, but this time, instead of parking out front, she took a right turn and followed a narrow drive to additional parking tucked behind a Chinese restaurant. This lot was nearly empty, and Nancy pulled her car into a space in the back corner.

She got out and made a quick visual check of her surroundings. Then, starting at the driver's side, Nancy began to work her way around the Mustang, feeling carefully under the front bumper and the wheel wells.

She was inching her way around the back bumper on the passenger's side when her fingers touched something hard and square.

Nancy pulled out a small, metal box with strong magnets on one side. She didn't need to examine it more. She knew it was a transmitter!

Chapter
Thirteen

No wonder she hadn't seen her tail, Nancy thought. The FBI had been tracking her electronically. She carefully replaced the box, wondering if Victor was good enough to know she had discovered his secret. There was no one in sight as she started toward Andy's Arcade.

"Nancy, we thought *you'd* been kidnapped," Bess said from the large, semicircular booth where she sat with George, Luke, and Sean. Across the room teens were working the levers at a bank of arcade games. "What happened to you?"

Nancy glanced at her watch and realized she was almost forty-five minutes late.

"We were about to send the FBI after you," George said, joking.

"That wouldn't have helped," Nancy said. "They were the reason I was late."

"Is there news?" Sean asked eagerly.

Nancy saw a young man in an Andy's Arcade apron start across the room toward them. She asked for fish 'n' chips and a soda and waited while each of her friends placed their orders. Then she told them about her visit to the FBI mobile command center and finding the transmitter on her car.

When the food arrived, George asked, "Want to go to the park after lunch? Luke's going to teach me how to throw a knuckleball."

Luke smiled over his double cheeseburger. "She's a natural. She'll pick it up easy."

"Let's all go," Nancy replied.

"I'm game," Bess agreed, daintily picking up a french fry.

"Leave me out." Sean frowned. "I'm going back home. Lunch is a nice break, but I really need to stay by the phone."

After that Sean remained silent, though when they left the restaurant he followed Nancy to her car.

"I'm getting scared," he said, his face pale. "If we lose the game tomorrow, the series will be over. The Rangers will have won, and the kidnappers won't need Caitlin anymore."

"Then Caitlin can come back home," Nancy said quietly.

"Maybe," Sean said. "But let's not forget that Caitlin probably knows who the kidnappers are. They might not let her go."

It was a possibility, unless Nancy could solve the case before the series was over.

"You could win the game," Nancy said. "Then the series would continue."

Sean frowned. "No, I can't—not when they've told me to lose." He wanted to say more, Nancy could tell, but couldn't.

"We'll find her," Nancy told him firmly. But after he'd gone, she couldn't help wondering if they would.

Twenty minutes later Bess and Nancy settled on the grass under an oak tree in River Park. Luke pulled George's Falcons cap down over her eyes and the two were quickly caught up in a game of chase, which Luke soon won, tackling George.

It was good to see someone having fun, Nancy thought. She and Bess watched as Luke leaned over George's shoulder, showing her how to hold the ball.

"I think I've got it." George laughed, holding the ball in the air with her knuckles aligned along the seams.

Luke backed up to catch George's pitches, which were clumsy at first.

"You've got to fire them in here," he urged as he tossed the ball back to her. "Come on, show me your stuff."

George made an exaggerated windup and then giggled when Luke had to run down her wild pitch.

Nancy remembered when Ned had brought her to this same park to show her how to throw a football. That seemed like ages ago. It would be nice to have him here now.

"That's it!" Luke yelled, jumping to his feet as one of George's pitches finally cooked. "You're not ready for the majors yet, but you've got the basics. Anyone for a soda?" he called, walking toward Nancy and Bess.

"Thanks, but I've got an interview to get ready for," Nancy said, checking her watch.

"I'm out, too," Bess said as they got to their feet.

"That leaves you," Luke said, turning to George with a grin.

"Sounds good to me," George said. "As long as you promise to call me if anything important happens, Nancy."

Nancy agreed, and George and Luke headed for his car hand-in-hand.

Nancy dropped off Bess and got to her house just as the phone was ringing. She answered it casually and was taken by surprise.

"Nancy?" It was Ned. "I was about to hang up."

"I'm glad you didn't," she said, sighing.

"What have you been up to?" he asked. "It seems like forever since we've talked. I bet you have another case by now."

"Of course," Nancy replied. "I had to do something to stay busy while you were gone." Then she told him about the kidnapping.

"So, tell me about Sean," Ned said. "He's supposed to be really something."

She could detect a touch of jealousy in his tone, and smiled. "Why don't you come home and meet him?"

"I thought you'd never ask," Ned said. "How does Thursday sound? They're letting me out of here a couple days early, and I think I can make it for the last game of the series."

"I just hope the Falcons don't lose it tomorrow," she said. "But let's think positively. It's a date."

Nancy hung up, praying that the kidnapping would be solved by then. She changed into a pair of slacks, a white blouse, and a jacket, and took a stenographer's pad and pencil from her father's desk. Then she left the house and drove to the River's Edge Lodge.

The restaurant was connected to the lobby. As soon as she pushed through the glass doors, she spotted Stormy. The Rangers owner was already at a round table in the center of the room. She was wearing black pants and a blue T-shirt with a picture of a cartoon cowboy stepping on a bird that looked a little like Freddy the Falcon.

Nancy introduced herself and pulled up a chair across from Stormy.

"I hope you're going to cover our victory tomorrow," Stormy said.

"You seem awfully confident," Nancy commented as she pulled her chair in. A large platter of boiled shrimp sat between them.

"I'm always confident," Stormy returned loudly, cracking open a shrimp and gulping it down. A few customers turned and frowned at her. "We're number one," she chanted, raising her arms to address the entire restaurant and succeeding only in antagonizing the other customers.

Nancy smiled.

"I understand you need this win," she said, putting her notebook on the table.

"Who doesn't need a win?" Stormy said, leaning close to Nancy. "It's what baseball's all about." And then as an afterthought she added, "Have some shrimp."

Nancy smiled but waved the food away. "The paper said this win is especially important to you," she pressed.

"You mean my money problems," Stormy answered, brushing her hand through the air as if to wave the comment away.

"What about them?" Nancy pressed. "Obviously, you've heard the rumors."

"Nonsense, absolute nonsense," Stormy said.

"Then you're not having financial problems?"

"Certainly not," Stormy snapped.

"And the television deal?"

"Bad question," Stormy said, dunking another shrimp in a bowl of hot sauce. "I'm not talking about TV tonight."

Nancy scribbled on her pad, to make her reporter disguise appear real. "I was watching you in the stands yesterday," Nancy said with a smile. "Do you always get to the games early?"

Stormy laughed heartily. "I try to," she said. "But sometimes it doesn't work out. Like Sunday when I had a flat tire on the way to the park. Can you believe it? I called my mechanic from the first pay phone I got to and told him heads would roll when I got back to Mill City."

Nancy made another note on her pad. She wondered whether Stormy was telling the truth. If she was, she had an alibi for the time when Caitlin was kidnapped.

Stormy waved to a waitress and ordered another plate of shrimp. "Enough about baseball," she said. "Let's talk about me. Did you know that when I was twelve, I hit more home runs than anyone else in my city league? But they wouldn't let me play once I got to high school. So as soon as I could, I bought myself a team."

Stormy continued chatting about herself while Nancy took notes obediently, hoping eventually to get back to more important subjects—such as whether Stormy had ever seen the inside of a Freddy the Falcon suit. She never got the chance.

Ten minutes later the waitress returned. "You have a phone call," she said to Stormy.

The Rangers' owner left the table without even excusing herself. She talked for only a few minutes at the phone on the hostess's desk, said a few words to the waitress, and headed out the door.

Nancy was on her feet in an instant. She caught

the waitress on her way to the kitchen. "Excuse me," she said politely. "Did Ms. Tarver say where she was going?"

"I'm afraid not," the waitress said. "But she did say you could have whatever you wanted and she'd pick up the tab."

Nancy was instantly suspicious. She spotted a door that led directly to the parking lot, went through it to her car, and watched the front entrance of the River's Edge Lodge.

About five minutes later she saw Stormy Tarver come out and slip behind the wheel of a black luxury sedan. Delgado had said the FBI was following Stormy, but Nancy couldn't take a chance. She was certain the Rangers' owner was on her way someplace important.

Nancy started up and pulled into traffic, following the black sedan.

Stormy turned right at the first intersection and drove north before turning again onto a quiet side street that wound through a residential area. She pulled to a stop at the edge of a park.

The park was just a block wide and about twice as long. Stormy parked near a bench. Behind it was a small rose garden and a grass-covered hillside that ended at the walk running alongside the next street.

Nancy rounded the end of the park and pulled into a lot on the upper edge. A row of trees and shrubs partially shielded her from Stormy. Guessing that Stormy was about to meet someone, she came up with a plan. She took the bag of clothes from the backseat and headed for the row of trees.

Stormy had taken a seat on the bench. Soon another car appeared, the vehicle stopped, and a man got out and approached the bench. Storm clouds had gathered, and the streetlights automatically came on. Nancy had to wait for the man to pass under a streetlight to identify him as Rod Sanders.

Nancy quickly pulled on her father's old top coat and traded her sandals for a pair of his worn tennis shoes. She had to lace the shoes extra tight to keep them on her feet. Next she stuffed her shiny hair up into a wide-brimmed hat. She dug through the bag and found a green scarf, which she pulled over the hat and knotted under her chin to help hide her face, then smudged some dirt on her cheeks.

Rod was almost to the bench now, so she turned the coat collar up and grabbed the paper bag. She glanced around the park one more time. There was no sign of the FBI.

Nancy began to shuffle down the concrete walk, keeping her eyes on the ground as though searching for trash or recyclables. She hoped Stormy and Rod would dismiss her as a bag lady, scavenging in the park.

Nancy felt a surge of adrenaline as she neared the bench where Stormy was sitting. She could hear the faint murmur of them talking. With great effort she kept her steps slow. As she approached, Nancy spotted a trash can beside the bench and headed straight for it, ignoring the two suspects.

"Don't get mad at me—you're the one who wanted the job," Stormy said, raising her voice slightly.

Nancy set her paper bag beside the trash can and began to rummage around inside it, trying hard to avoid the worst of the garbage.

"I don't like seeing you during the series. Someone might spot us," Rod said as Nancy pulled an aluminum can from the trash and dropped it into her bag. She could hardly believe her ears.

"No more notes and no more phone calls," he went on. Nancy pulled her head out of the garbage can, so she could hear Stormy's response. She was so focused on her suspects that she accidentally kicked her bag. It fell over in a loud crash, and Stormy swung around to stare at her.

Nancy's heart skipped a beat.

If either of them recognized her, Sean might never see his daughter again.

Chapter

Fourteen

"WATCH IT!" Nancy said, pretending to accuse them of knocking the bag over. Once again she leaned into the can and began rummaging through the garbage.

"Sorry," Rod said, obviously thinking she was crazy.

Nancy didn't react but continued to paw garbage for several minutes before pulling her head out of the can. The bench was empty. Stormy was already in her car, and Rod was halfway to his, covering the distance with long, angry strides.

Nancy breathed a sigh of relief. She picked up her paper bag and started back toward her car, giving up the slow shuffle as soon as Stormy and Rod had driven away.

Nancy was walking past the row of shrubs when she heard a voice.

"Is there anything you don't do?"

Nancy jumped, but then relaxed when Victor Delgado came out from his hiding place in the bushes. He studied her from head to toe, smiled, and shook his head slowly.

"It was the best I could manage on short notice," Nancy said wryly.

"You could have caused real problems with that stunt," Delgado said. "What if they had recognized you?"

"But they didn't," Nancy said. "And wait until I tell you what they said."

Victor followed Nancy back to her car and listened carefully as she repeated Rod's words while taking off her disguise.

"They're definitely in on something together," Nancy said.

"You're right." Victor took a deep breath and let it out slowly. "And we wouldn't have gotten it without you. More than that, what you did took guts. I guess it's time to tell you that you're a good detective, Nancy Drew."

"That's nice to hear from the FBI," Nancy said, smiling. "You're not bad yourself. Now, what are we going to do about Caitlin?"

"Unfortunately, we still have to let our suspects make the next move," Victor said. "Even if Rod and Stormy are involved, we don't have anything on them that would stand up in court. And if we arrested them now, they could refuse to talk, meaning we might never find Sean's daughter."

"So we just keep waiting and hope one of them leads us to Caitlin?"

"I'm afraid so," Victor answered. "In the meantime, I think I'll get some sleep. Following you has worn me out."

It was just a few minutes past one the next afternoon when Nancy left her house for the Falcon's Roost. She had spent a good part of the morning on the phone giving updates to George and Bess, whom she was meeting at the stadium. She knew George would have filled Luke in, and Victor had promised to talk to Sean. Nancy had also spoken with Chief McGinnis and been assured that Delgado's men were watching both Rod and Stormy.

"Nothing yet," McGinnis had said. "But we'll find Caitlin soon, Nancy, and it will be thanks in large part to you."

The praise, first from Victor, and then from Chief McGinnis, had felt good, but Nancy couldn't help thinking that it was premature. As she drove toward the stadium, she kept hearing Sean's words in her mind.

"If we lose tomorrow, the series will be over," he had said. "The kidnappers won't need Caitlin anymore."

Tomorrow had come. In just half an hour the game would start. Stormy and Rod were her prime suspects, but not the only ones. She hadn't found anything much on Rebecca. If she was involved, who was helping her?

Her brain boiling over with questions, Nancy brought her Mustang to a halt at the same red light where she had avoided a collision on her way to the second game of the series.

She shifted her car into reverse and eased it back to make room for a flatbed truck trying to make a wide turn. It was empty, and Nancy guessed it was a lumber truck coming back from a construction site west of town.

As the truck squeaked past the front fender of her Mustang, Nancy noticed something. Mashed into the tires of the truck were mounds of soft gray clay.

The possibility that it was from the same place as the clay she'd seen at Sean's house was a long shot, Nancy knew, and even if she had wanted to chase it down, this truck was coming back from the site, not going to it. She was considering a way to find the source of the clay when a concrete truck whizzed through the intersection heading out of town. Nancy seized the opportunity and pulled in behind it. The Falcon's Roost could wait, she decided.

The street soon narrowed from four lanes to two, and sidewalks gave way to gravel shoulders. Nancy was beginning to wonder if she was on a wild-goose chase when the truck slowed and pulled into an unpaved drive at a barren construction site. On one side of the site stood a large stack of lumber and out front a sign declared, Future Home of Marshall Manufacturing.

Nancy pulled her car to the shoulder of the road and got out. There was clay in the ruts of the driveway, but there was no building big enough to hide a child in. She got back in her car and drove past the construction site, taking a side road that led toward the back of the lot. It had deep ruts and was partially overgrown with weeds. About a hundred yards along Nancy stopped and got out of her car. There was gray clay on this road, too, and some of the weeds had been crushed as though a vehicle had recently gone through.

Nancy surveyed the land. The construction site was on her left now. To the right were open fields, and straight ahead the dirt road disappeared into a large stand of trees and heavy brush. A good place for a hideout, she thought, but if she was going to investigate, it would have to be on foot. In her car she couldn't hope to take anyone by surprise.

Nancy got back in her car and inched it forward. When she was close to the trees, she pulled off the dirt track, parked in the weeds, and continued down the road on foot.

She checked the ground again and found more gray clay in the ruts of the road. All her instincts told her she was on the right track. As she walked carefully along the edge of the road, her only wish was that Victor was still tailing her. She wondered if the workers at the construction site would hear her if she called for help. She guessed they wouldn't, and as the trees thickened, Nancy was very aware that she was on her own.

Her nerves were on edge when she came to the end of the road. It stopped at a small clearing, barely large enough to turn a car around in. There, pointed straight at her, was a battered green sedan—the very kind Sean had said Rebecca owned. Nancy walked up to it and peered in the window. Inside, on the floor of the backseat, were a tattered doll and an empty Yummy Bunnies box.

Caitlin! The word was a silent scream inside Nancy's head. She was sure now that the little girl was close, but where? Nancy scanned the clearing and spotted a narrow path heading off to the right. It led to a small, run-down cottage. What had once been a driveway was now overgrown, but the grass around the front door had been trampled.

Nancy watched from the trees for a moment and then edged her way toward the rickety front porch. She was about to climb the steps when the front door opened. Nancy held her breath as a red-haired young woman led a small child onto the porch. Nancy recognized them immediately from their pictures as Rebecca and Caitlin.

The baby-sitter gasped.

"Good afternoon," Nancy said, acting friendly.

Rebecca pulled Caitlin to her, then froze. "What do you want?"

Nancy hesitated. She wasn't going home without Caitlin, but she didn't want to frighten Rebecca into doing something desperate.

"I was just looking around," Nancy said with a smile. "I thought there might be a stream in these trees—and then I saw your cottage."

"I'm afraid there's no stream," Rebecca said tersely. "Now, if you'll excuse me, we're in a hurry." She pulled the door closed and led Caitlin down the steps, turning her back on Nancy.

Nancy saw her opportunity. "Run, Caitlin!" she yelled as she lunged at Rebecca. She pushed Caitlin aside as she threw her forearm around the kidnapper's neck. Instantly Rebecca jerked forward, flipping Nancy onto her back on the hard ground.

Before Nancy could catch her breath, Rebecca had her foot on Nancy's chest. "Who are you?" she growled.

Chapter

Fifteen

Nancy raised her eyes in time to see Rebecca glaring down at her, her foot digging hard into Nancy's chest. Before she could say anything, Caitlin began to sob.

"You said you'd take me home," the little girl wailed. "I want to go home."

Rebecca glanced toward the child, giving Nancy the opportunity she needed. She quickly twisted out from under Rebecca's heel, grabbing the kidnapper's leg and pulling hard. Rebecca came down heavily as Nancy sprang up. Now the tables were turned—Nancy was standing over Rebecca, with her foot on the sitter's stomach.

"I'm a friend of Sean Reeves, and I'm here to take Caitlin home," she said.

Behind her she heard Caitlin cry, "I want my daddy!"

"Caitlin," Nancy said as she twisted toward the sobbing child. "I'll take you to your daddy, but I need your help first."

The little girl wiped her tears away with dirty hands.

"Do you know where there's a rope?" Nancy asked.

Caitlin immediately began to sniffle.

"It's not for you," Nancy said, keeping a sharp eye on Rebecca. "I promise. I just need you to bring it to me."

Caitlin hesitated, her eyes growing wide. Finally she walked slowly up the steps of the cottage and disappeared inside. When she returned, she had a piece of clothesline in her hand, which she dropped in front of Nancy.

It took Nancy only a few minutes to tie Rebecca's hands. Nancy forced her through the trees toward her car. Caitlin followed several paces behind them.

"You'd better let me go," Rebecca commanded as Nancy pushed her along. "If you do, I won't tell the cops how you tied me up and kidnapped me."

"You're the kidnapper," Nancy said. "And it will be better for you if you tell me all about it."

"I'm not telling you anything," Rebecca snapped.

"How about who your accomplice was," Nancy said as they neared the Mustang. "I know you couldn't have pulled this off all by yourself."

"I want a lawyer," Rebecca said flatly. Nancy

shoved her into the backseat and tied her feet. She had already decided to take Rebecca to the FBI mobile command center. She was anxious to get to the Roost, and the police department was too far out of her way.

Nancy glanced at her watch and realized the game was already well under way. She would have to hurry to get word to Sean before he threw another game.

"Your dad's been looking for you," Nancy said gently as she helped Caitlin into the car. "Have you been at that cottage the whole time?"

"Uh-huh," Caitlin said, her big brown eyes fixed on Nancy. "She wouldn't even let me go outside, and it got really boring once the Yummy Bunnies were gone."

"Did she hurt you?" Nancy asked, reaching out to stroke Caitlin's hair gently.

"Just when they took me away from the house," Caitlin said. "I didn't want to go."

"Were you sleeping?" Nancy asked.

"No. It was right after Dad left, and I was playing with my dolls," Caitlin said. "But then a man came and started throwing things around the house. I cried and Rebecca took me to her car on the side of the house."

Nancy shook her head grimly and sighed. Obviously Rebecca had been in on the kidnapping all along. Caitlin *hadn't* been taken from her bed while she napped between twelve-thirty and one-thirty. She had actually been kidnapped much earlier in the day, and the house had been deliberately wrecked to make it look as if there had been a struggle.

"Caitlin, what did the man look like?" Nancy asked, keeping her voice gentle.

"He was big," Caitlin said.

"What color hair did he have?" Nancy asked.

"I don't remember," Caitlin said. "Besides, he had a hat on. It was blue."

A big man in a blue hat. Not much to go on, Nancy thought. "Would you know him if you saw him again?" Nancy asked Caitlin, hopefully.

"Yes," Caitlin said without hesitation. "He was mean. He broke the flowers I cut for daddy."

"Good," Nancy said. "I have a plan." She knew there was still not enough evidence to arrest Rod or Stormy, but she had an idea that might flush Rebecca's accomplice out. To make it work, she had to get to the Roost before Sean took over for the starting pitcher.

When she reached the city limits, Nancy steered her car toward the parking lot where Victor had sent her the day before. As she rounded the corner, Nancy saw that she was in luck. The FBI's mobile command unit was still there. She pulled up beside it and got out of the car.

"Where are we?" Rebecca demanded as Nancy opened the back door.

"We're going to have a little visit with the FBI," Nancy said, untying Rebecca's feet.

"The FBI?" Rebecca said with disbelief. For

the first time Nancy saw real fear in her eyes. "Look, I—I didn't mean for this to be such a big deal," she stammered.

Nancy pulled her out of the car and led her to the door of the van. She knocked, then stepped aside as the door swung open and Victor peered out. He acted shocked as his eyes moved from Nancy to Rebecca to Caitlin.

"A little present," Nancy said, smiling. "Meet Rebecca Carter and Caitlin Reeves."

Victor called to his assistant, who quickly read Rebecca her rights and took her inside the van.

"I guess I stopped following you too soon," he said to Nancy. "I'm going to need to know exactly what happened."

"I'll be glad to tell you," she answered with a smile. "But right now I'd like to get to the Roost so I can stop Sean from throwing another game."

"I'm all for that," Victor agreed.

"And since Rebecca's not talking, we still need to force her accomplice into the open. If Sean starts pitching well, he or she may get nervous," Nancy said. "But it might be even easier than that. Caitlin saw the man who helped kidnap her. She can't give much of a description, but she's a bright little girl. I think she could recognize him."

"That would be enough for an arrest warrant," Victor said. "Let's give it a try."

"Will you help us?" Nancy asked, looking down at Caitlin.

The little girl gripped Nancy's hand and nodded. "Then can I see my daddy?" she asked.

"You bet," Nancy said with a gentle smile.

"Let's go, then," Victor urged. He scrambled into the backseat of Nancy's car. Nancy helped Caitlin into the front seat again, and within moments the three of them were on their way to the Roost.

"Good work!" Chief McGinnis said when Nancy got out of her car in the stadium parking lot. "I heard all about it on my police radio and came right over."

Nancy quickly explained her plan to the chief.

"If we're in time, Victor can talk to Sean before he goes onto the field," Nancy said.

"And I'll find the mascot," McGinnis said.

The four of them hurried toward the entrance. Chief McGinnis showed his badge to the young woman taking tickets, and all four passed quickly through the gates.

Nancy took Caitlin's hand and headed toward the section of the stands where she and George had sat at both games earlier that week. She was just about to start up the ramp when she heard a familiar voice.

"I think you know more than you've been telling, Nancy Drew, and I'm going to stay with you till I get the whole story."

Nancy turned around to see Brenda hurrying to catch up to her.

"I really mean it," Brenda said. "I'm going to stick to you like glue."

Nancy couldn't believe Brenda's timing. She had to think of a way to get rid of the reporter, and fast.

"I promise to tell you everything after the game if you'll leave me alone for now," Nancy said, trying to smile.

"Then you do have a story!" Brenda exclaimed.

"Yes, and it will be worth the wait," Nancy said. "But you have to agree not to follow me."

Brenda peeked at Caitlin and then back at Nancy. "Agreed, if I get an exclusive."

Nancy just nodded and led Caitlin up the ramp. It took her only a few minutes to find George sitting next to an empty seat. Before Nancy could speak, George's mouth fell open.

"You found her!" George gasped. "And in time for Sean to pitch his best."

"Yes, but right now we need your help," Nancy said. George quickly followed her and Caitlin back down the aisle and up a long flight of steps to the stadium announcer's box overlooking home plate while Nancy explained her plan. On the field Sean Reeves walked to the pitcher's mound.

"Do you really think the kidnapper will try to get another message to Sean when he starts pitching well?" George asked.

"I hope so," Nancy said. "But it's possible we

can wrap this case up before then if Caitlin can finger Rebecca's accomplice."

Nancy continued up the steps. "What's happening in the game?"

"It's tied!" George said excitedly. "Four to four in the top of the seventh inning. The Falcons could win."

"Maybe so," Nancy said with a smile and stopped in front of the steel door to the booth. She knocked softly. When a young man answered it, she explained what she needed.

A moment later Nancy, George, and Caitlin were inside the crowded room.

Al Wickenhagen, "the Voice of the Falcons," was giving game details over the stadium P.A. system. Nancy asked Caitlin to speak very quietly so that they would not be heard over Wickenhagen's microphone. She settled down in a folding chair beside the announcer and pulled Caitlin onto her lap. It was easy to see that Sean had gotten the word that his daughter was safe, because he was throwing killer fastballs.

"Is that my daddy?" Caitlin asked, pointing to the pitcher's mound.

Nancy nodded. Nothing could be better than seeing the two of them back together again, she thought.

"There's another strikeout," Wickenhagen bellowed into the microphone next to them. "That's two in a row for Reeves."

"I think his tune-up is complete," George whispered. "If the kidnapper is still hoping for a Ranger victory, he has to be a little worried right about now."

"Let's hope so," Nancy said as the Rangers' third batter hit a pop fly for the third out of the inning.

The first Falcon batter was coming to the plate when the light on the telephone between Nancy and the announcer started flashing.

The young man who'd met them at the door picked it up, spoke into it softly, then handed it to Nancy. "It's for you," he told her.

"Victor?" Nancy said as she took the receiver.

"None other," the agent replied.

"What's up?" Nancy asked. She could feel the excitement building within her.

"Rod Sanders didn't suit up today," Victor said. "He's in the stands, Section G, Row eighteen. There are plainclothes officers near both him and Stormy, and we've got officers posted at all the exits."

Nancy was stunned. Rod was sitting on the Ranger side of the stadium. She thanked Victor, hung up, and began counting the rows in Section G. When she got to eighteen, she used binoculars to search the faces until she found Rod.

Nancy grinned as she wondered which of the people in the stands near him were FBI agents.

"Is that the man who took you?" Nancy asked Caitlin after helping her spot Rod.

Caitlin looked for a moment and then shook her head.

"Are you sure?" Nancy asked, surprised.

"That's not him," Caitlin insisted.

Nancy was stunned. As the inning's second batter hit a long line drive and scored a run that put the Falcons in the lead, she wondered who the kidnapper could be. Maybe Stormy Tarver, dressed up like a man, she thought.

It was easy to locate Stormy in the box where she had spent every day of the series, but it took several minutes to point her out to Caitlin. The inning was over and Sean was again on the mound when Caitlin finally shook her head. "The man who came and got me had dirt on his face."

Nancy looked at Caitlin and then at George, who shrugged.

"A brown mark right here?" she whispered to Caitlin, touching her right cheek.

"Uh-huh," Caitlin said.

"A birthmark," she said to George over her shoulder. "The kidnapper has a birthmark—and so does Bill Barrows."

"Caitlin, would you like to say hello to your dad?" Wickenhagen whispered.

Caitlin leaned as close as she could to the announcer's mike. "Hello, Daddy," she said loudly.

Wickenhagen introduced her to the fans. Nancy scanned the field to see Sean staring up at the announcer's booth. Then, halfway between the pitcher's mound and the Falcons' dugout, she spotted Freddy the Falcon, frozen in his tracks.

The FBI was following the wrong suspects. Bill Barrows was the kidnapper, and he was already on the field!

Chapter

Sixteen

Nancy watched from the announcer's stand long enough to see the mascot run awkwardly to center field with Sean chasing him. Luke threw off his catcher's mitt and joined the pursuit.

"Stay with George," Nancy said to Caitlin as she lifted the girl to the floor and dashed out of the booth. She headed down the steps, listening as the crowd roared with laughter. Once again the spectators thought what was going on was part of the show.

At the bottom of the first section of steps, Nancy stopped to watch Sean dive for Freddy the Falcon and come up with only a handful of feathers. The huge blue and green bird was making mad weaving dashes around the bases, trying to stay out of the reach of his pursuers.

Nancy dashed down more flights of stairs. She'd almost reached field level when she paused at a landing to check the action. The mascot had dodged toward the bat rack by the Falcons' dugout. Nancy saw him hurl one of the bats right at Luke's head.

"Duck!" Nancy screamed. Then, realizing that she was too far from the field to be heard, she took off again, flying down the last flight of stairs. She reached the ramp that led to the playing field just as Freddy the Falcon grabbed another bat and began to swing it at Sean. The pitcher's eyes were blazing with anger.

"No, Sean!" Nancy yelled as she ran down the ramp toward the barrier that separated the stands from the field. Sean lunged but just missed the dodging bird, falling to the ground as the mascot jumped the barrier several aisles down from Nancy and tore up the ramp.

Nancy heard "Drop it!" from the corridor. She dashed back to the inside of the stadium in time to see the bat-wielding Falcon mascot facing an empty-handed Victor Delgado.

Already a few curious spectators were peering around corners in the corridor. Nancy knew that Victor would risk his own life before he'd pull a gun in this situation.

"Put it down," Victor said again.

Nancy glanced around for some kind of weapon but spotted nothing. Her only hope was that with the costume on, Barrows wouldn't see her coming from behind. She took two swift steps toward him and used a roundhouse kick to knock both his feet out from under him.

141

Feathers flew as the mascot threw the bat into the air and crashed to the ground on his shoulders.

Nancy was quickly on top of him.

"Good work," Victor said, finally pulling his gun and training it on Barrows. "Now let's see who this guy really is."

"It's Bill Barrows," Nancy replied smoothly. "Caitlin remembered his birthmark." With that, she grabbed a handful of fabric and feathers on each side of the mascot's head and pulled.

"You're right again, Nancy Drew," Victor said as the feather costume gave way to reveal an angry Bill Barrows.

Nancy noticed Sean and Luke staring down at him.

"I suppose you have an explanation for this," Victor said to the pinned man.

"For what?" Barrows snapped. "Wearing a mascot costume at a baseball game?"

"For kidnapping," Victor said soberly, pulling Barrows to his feet. "And extortion."

"But why would you want your own team to lose?" Sean blurted out, his face red with anger. "And why did you take my daughter?"

"Is money a good enough reason for you?" Barrows snapped as Victor handcuffed his wrists behind him.

"But there was no ransom demand," Nancy said.

"I made a bet on the series," Barrows shot back defiantly. "I bet the Rangers would win.

And they would have, if Sean hadn't shown up. He was about to ruin everything, and I had orders to play him three innings a game no matter what. When he hired Rebecca to baby-sit, I knew it would be easy. She likes money as much as anybody."

"So you knew she used to work for the Falcons?" Nancy asked.

"Yeah, I keep an eye on the personnel files."

Nancy was watching Barrows's face when she heard Sean gasp.

"Daddy!" Caitlin yelled.

She turned to see the little girl and George breaking through the crowd that had gathered around them.

"Caitlin!" Sean cried. Before he could run to her, the girl had broken free from George and dashed across the concrete floor. She leaped through the air and landed in her father's arms.

"Oh, Caitlin, you're safe," Sean said as he wrapped his arms around her.

Cries of approval rose from the crowd. Sean lifted his head to see the spectators smiling warmly and clapping their hands. They didn't really understand what was happening, Nancy knew, but the affection between Sean and his daughter was so strong that it was hard for anyone to keep from cheering.

Finally Sean lowered Caitlin to the ground and placed her hand gently in Nancy's. "Daddy has one more thing to do," he said, squatting down to look Caitlin in the eye. "Is that okay?"

Caitlin nodded bravely and, guessing what it was, added, "Pitch good, Daddy."

Sean tousled her hair as he rose to his feet and motioned to Luke. "Come on," he said. "We have a game to win."

More applause rose from the spectators, who then quickly returned to the stands as Luke and Sean marched onto the field.

Nancy and George led Caitlin back to their front row seats to watch the end of the game.

"Do you think they can do it?" George asked as they took their seats.

"I hope so," said Nancy.

Sean threw strike after strike, retiring one batter after another in both the eighth and ninth innings.

Luke added a two-run homer to clinch the Falcons' victory. The league championship would come down to the fifth game on Thursday.

The sun was setting on Thursday evening when George, Nancy, and Ned walked onto the baseball field where the River Heights Falcons were accepting the league championship trophy.

"That was a great game," Ned said as they showed their special passes to the attendant at the entrance to the playing field.

"And great company," Nancy added, smiling up at her handsome boyfriend. "I'm glad you got home in time to see the Falcons win."

"And I'm glad your case is wrapped up," he

said. "Maybe we'll finally get some time together."

"I'd like that," Nancy replied.

"Am I too late?" Bess called from behind them. "Carolyn said she'd clean up tonight so I could watch the awards. I'm hoping to see Sean smile. I bet he's a knockout when he smiles."

"You never change, do you, Bess?" Nancy couldn't help but grin as she shook her head at her friend.

"And I bet you don't, either, Nancy Drew."

Nancy turned around to see Victor Delgado wearing a stylish business suit with a forest-green tie. His dark hair was neatly combed and he looked very much like the all-business FBI agents Nancy was used to seeing on the news. He stood beside her on the grassy field.

"I just wanted to say it's been good working with you," Victor said. "And if you ever want to join the FBI, call me. I'll give you a great recommendation."

"Thank you," Nancy said, blushing a little.

"By the way, we found out that Barrows bet seventy-five thousand dollars that the Falcons would lose the series, and that he got Rebecca to help by promising to share the winnings with her," Victor said. "Barrows helped get Caitlin into Rebecca's car and then followed them to the hideout. That's also where Barrows cut the lock of hair from Caitlin. Unfortunately for them, they were both at the hideout on the morning before the kidnapping. Barrows tracked clay to Sean's, and Rebecca left some at the side entrance and on her own doorstep. She dropped her shopping list near her car when she was putting Caitlin in."

"But why did Barrows get into the Freddy the Falcon uniform?" Bess asked. "Why didn't he just tell Sean what he wanted over the phone?"

"Barrows said he was hoping Sean's pitching would be so bad, he wouldn't have to make the threat at all," Victor said. "Then there would have been even fewer clues to connect him to the crime."

"What about the phone calls to the manager's office?" George asked.

"Rebecca made them on a cellular phone. She pretended to be upset the first time. The second time Barrows just said it was a man's voice to throw Sean off the track," Victor said.

"And we decided Barrows couldn't be a suspect because he was at the stadium when we thought Caitlin was taken," Bess remarked.

"But the kidnapping really happened right after Sean left the house, which gave Barrows time to get to the stadium before he did," Nancy explained.

"It was pretty stupid of Barrows to steal the mascot costume a second time," Bess commented. "And what about poor Anthony Reyes?"

"Chief McGinnis tried to find him as soon as we got to the game yesterday, but it was too late.

Barrows had already gotten to him, knocked him out, and taken the costume again," Victor said. "Criminals tend to repeat themselves," he added, shaking his head. "It's strange."

"Is Anthony all right?" George asked.

"Yes," Victor said. "And we'll be able to put Rebecca and Barrows away for a long time. It's all thanks to you," he added, turning to Nancy.

He shook her hand, said goodbye, and then disappeared into the crowd. Nancy wondered if Brenda would get more details about the case from him. Probably not, she decided. Brenda wasn't very thorough, and she'd already scored a victory of her own with the article she'd written for that morning's paper.

A cheer went up from the crowd as the silver-haired league president carried a large trophy and a microphone onto the field. He was quickly surrounded by Falcon players, with Sean and Rod at the front of the crowd. Both players had pitched excellent games that day, cementing the series victory. As the league president held out their trophy, each of them took one handle of the large silver cup and held it skyward.

"We want to thank all the people who made this victory possible," Rod said, holding the microphone. "Especially one young detective whom I'm sure you read about in this morning's paper."

A murmur ran through the crowd and Nancy felt her cheeks flush with embarrassment.

The Falcon players stepped back as Stormy Tarver pushed through the crowd to accept the second-place trophy.

"It was a good series, but it would have been better if we'd won," Stormy said. Laughter rose from the crowd. "Next year I'm going to take two things away from River Heights. The championship and Rod Sanders! He's agreed to be the Rangers' new pitching coach."

Nancy and George exchanged looks. That explained what Rod and Stormy had been talking about when they met in the park. Nancy could understand why he hadn't wanted the word to get out during the series. He would have looked like a traitor.

Stormy had just left when Luke broke through the crowd and came to George's side.

"Great hitting," George said. She held out her hand with her palm up, and Luke slapped it. "With stats like yours you'll be on your way to the majors in no time."

Nancy smiled at the two of them. George and Luke had a lot in common, and this time it didn't make Nancy feel lonely to see them together. She slipped her hand into Ned's.

"If I do, there'll be somebody there I know," Luke said. "Sean's been called back to the Captains. There was a coach here today who seems to think his pitching problems are all worked out."

"That's an understatement," George said, smiling up at Luke.

Nancy felt a tap on her shoulder and turned to see Caitlin riding on her dad's shoulders.

"Caitlin has a message for you from both of us," Sean said.

"Daddy and I think you're a good 'tective and we're glad you found me," Caitlin said brightly. Then she held out a handful of multicolored Yummy Bunnies.

"Thanks," Nancy said, taking the cookies. She popped one in her mouth and smiled up at the brown-eyed girl. It had been an amazing baseball series. In fact, Nancy hoped that she'd never see another one as exciting.

Nancy's next case:

Behind the rustic charm of beautiful Block Island lurks an ugly secret . . . a secret worth killing for. The mystery began when Nancy joined grad student Barb Sommers on her summer fieldwork—and made a deadly discovery. Nancy may be able to help Barb, but there's nothing she can do for fisherman Tom Haines, victim of murder!

Haines was not a nice guy. An operator and a hustler, he was always on the lookout for a big score. But he got in too deep and paid with his life, leaving behind an island full of suspects. Now it's Nancy's turn to stir up the waters . . . and she's sure to stir up trouble. A killer's on the loose, and Nancy's swimming with the sharks . . . in *Island of Secrets,* Case #98 in The Nancy Drew Files™.